# OUTSIDE RULES

## Other Persea Anthologies

AMERICA STREET
A Multicultural Anthology of Stories
*Edited by Anne Mazer*

BIG CITY COOL
Short Stories About Urban Youth
*Edited by M. Jerry Weiss and Helen S. Weiss*

FISHING FOR CHICKENS
Short Stories About Rural Youth
*Edited by Jim Heynen*

GOING WHERE I'M COMING FROM
Memoirs of American Youth
*Edited by Anne Mazer*

STARTING WITH "I"
Personal Essays by Teenagers
*Youth Communication, Edited by Andrea Estepa
and Philip Kay*

A WALK IN MY WORLD
International Short Stories About Youth
*Edited by Anne Mazer*

WORKING DAYS
Short Stories About Teenagers at Work
*Edited by Anne Mazer*

Short Stories About
Nonconformist Youth

# OUTSIDE RULES

Edited, with an introduction by
**CLAIRE ROBSON**

A Karen and Michael Braziller Book
**PERSEA BOOKS / NEW YORK**

For permission to reprint and for any other information, write to the publisher:
Persea Books, Inc.
853 Broadway
New York, New York 10003

Library of Congress Cataloging-in-Publication Data
Outside rules : short stories about nonconformist youth / edited, with an introduction by Claire Robson.—1st ed.
     v. cm.
"A Karen and Michael Braziller Book."
     Summary: An anthology of fourteen short stories about youth who do not
quite fit in because they are too brainy, unathletic, poor, the "wrong" religion,
emotionally fragile, from non-traditional families, not model-thin, or simply
bent on following a unique path.
Contents: A minstrel visits / Sandell Morse—Mr.Softee / Wally
Lamb—My Tocaya / Sandra Cisneros—[etc.]
     ISBN 0-89255-316-2 (original trade pbk. : alk. paper)
     1. Short stories, American. 2. Short stories, English.
[1. Conformity—Fiction. 2. Social isolation—Fiction. 3. Interpersonal rela-
tions—Fiction. 4. Short stories.] I. Robson, Claire, 1949– .
     PZ7.O942 2006
     [Fic]—dc22                                            2006022548

Designed by Rita Lascaro
Manufactured in the United States of America
First Edition

# Contents

# Introduction

I was a kid who didn't fit in—too skinny, too wild, too weird. I have to say, though, looking back, I wouldn't change a thing. Being on the outside looking in sharpened both my powers of observation and my sense of humor. It toughened me up. Besides, why would anyone strive to be just like everyone else? Though being different can be humiliating, it can also be the opposite. Outsiders are special—they have gifts and talents that can be the source of envy and admiration. In this collection, I wanted to give a voice to all these outsiders. I wanted this collection to stick up for young people who are singled out because they don't behave, look, worship, or love they way they "should."

I was in for a big surprise. What I learned from reading so many stories on the topic is that we're all outsiders when it comes down to it. There's a place in every single one of us that is lonely and misunderstood. Check it out. Just say the word "outsider" to someone. There's instant illumination, like shining a flashlight into a deep, sad place in the collective memory. From bus drivers to bankers, kids to crones, we've all been there. We don't feel like outsiders because we're "too this" or "too that" ("dumb," "smart," "fat," "thin"—you fill in the blanks). We feel like outsiders because it's part of the human condition to feel alone.

That's why the buzz about this collection spread so quickly. The modest little email I sent out to my writer friends traveled as if by magic to classrooms, writing groups, newsletters, and bulletin boards all over the country. At that time, my mailbox was a dented and rusty affair, screwed to a huge maple tree just across the road from my house. Soon it was stuffed with manila envelopes on a daily basis. One of the first stories to turn up was "A Minstrel Visits" by Sandell Morse.

I saw at once that Susan, the main character, would feel right at home in this collection. Her deliberate grumpy frumpishness is a constant source of disappointment to her controlling, snobby mother, who would clearly have preferred a totally different kind of daughter—someone much more artsy and graceful. Susan's best defense is her refusal to care about her mother's opinion. Her mother is disgusted because Susan's overweight? So what! However, despite her air of bulletproof independence, Susan is a true outsider, lonely at heart and hungry for approval. Enter Peter, who's as quirky as Susan herself, but older and more strategic. He's learned—to use the imagery of the story—to roll with the punches. During his brief visit, Peter recognizes Susan's intelligence and determination, and gives her the confidence she needs to hurl herself (quite literally) back into life.

In contrast with Susan, Eli, the hero of Wally Lamb's story "Mr. Softee," has a lot going for him. He "sort of looks like Derek on *All My Children*" and has just landed the perfect summer job. He rejects the attentions of Doris, the local misfit, despite the fact that she's smart, perceptive, tough, and principled. Eli ignores her praising of his poem, "Identity," about "a guy... trying to decide who he really was." It's a sad irony that Doris could probably have helped him toward some understanding of that crucial issue. In his haste to distance himself from any hint of "weirdness" (and to impress the gorgeous Charlene), Eli loses touch with that finest part of himself—his integrity. The end of the story leaves him distanced from his father, his friends, and himself.

Marie, in "The White Room" by Rebecca Rule, is a little like Eli in that she tries to escape her artistic nature; it's just too scary, too much of a challenge. With the help of her mother, her uncle, and a spunky squirrel, however, she finally begins to paint, and by the end of the story she's lost in her art, "painting the life she knew." I liked this story's implication that although the creative impulse may bite (like Marie's squirrel) and even scar those who try to seize it, it is ultimately a "gift that cannot be contained."

The same theme is picked up in "My *Tocaya*" by Sandra Cisneros. Patricia Benavidez, an aspiring actress, seems doomed by the circumstances of her birth. Though Patricia wears "rhinestone earrings and glitter high heels to school" and adopts a phony English accent, the reality of her life is relentless toil in her father's greasy taco restaurant. I loved reading about the novel way she escapes.

These three stories—by Wally Lamb, Rebecca Rule, and Sandra Cisneros—speak to the power of creativity, which may set us apart, but at the same time, can provide us with the courage and the wit we need to survive.

Far from being wimps and victims, the outsiders in this collection have both guts and ingenuity. A great example is Shala, in K. Kvashay-Boyle's "Saint Chola." From the opening of this story—her first day in junior high—Shala seizes the initiative to name herself, to define herself in her own terms. There are real risks involved for any student who chooses not to conform—as Shala puts it, "you could get jacked up, beat up, messed up." In Shala's case, the fact that she is Muslim puts her at special risk—especially in an America lost in the frenzy of war. This story is full of ironies. At the same time as Shala's Muslim brother is at risk in Pakistan for looking "too American," Shala accidentally ends up looking "too Muslim" in America by wearing a hijab at her cousin's urging. Again ironically, the more that Shala's well-intentioned friends and their feminist moms tell her to take it off, the more she wants to wear it. Instead of making Shala "less," the hijab makes her "more"—a fine example of someone who defines herself and makes her own choices when it comes to her cultural heritage, rather than let others decide who she is. Once she's made those choices, she's ready to defend them.

A great story can let you walk in those proverbial "other shoes," let you see and experience things you'd never normally experience. Sometimes this represents a real challenge to the reader—those shoes can pinch a little! Discomfort encourages us to grow and change however, to buy bigger shoes, and in my book, that's one of the objectives of any work of art. I hope you are challenged by some of these stories.

Katharine Noel's gritty and painfully honest story, "April" is a great example. All too often, we pretend that mental illness doesn't exist, but here Noel brings the reality of it—the shame and stigma—right into front and center. I don't think anyone could be unmoved by Angie's grim struggle to hold it all together when her best friend visits.

Another tough story is "Surrounded by Sleep" by Akhil Sharma. It's true that many readers, even the young, have endured the plain uncomplicated grief of losing someone they love. However, as we follow the twists and turns of Ajay's feelings about his brother's accident, we learn that loss can be complicated. We also find out just how invisible, guilty, and isolated children can feel when parents focus on one sibling, even when the reasons are understandable.

Danny, in Rand Richards Cooper's story "Laughing in the Dark" has also lost a sibling—a sister who ran away from home and disappeared. As a result, Danny is quietly "falling through the cracks" as Mr. Latimer, his teacher, puts it. I'm sure Danny's not alone in his feeling that life is quietly unraveling this way. Even when adults like Mr. Latimer notice, they're often powerless to help. This story speaks to the value of having one good ally, in this case, the unlikely Angela Tourtelotte, with her honking laugh and outspoken Retro Punk act. I liked this story for the compassion it showed to everyone concerned. It's sad and funny and tender, and in the end, it's all about kindness.

I wanted this collection, above all else, to be relevant to young people. Imagine my delight when an elegant story written by a fifteen-year-old turned up in my mailbox! A creative writing teacher in Connecticut had heard about the project and encouraged one of his students, Caitlin Jeffrey Lonning, to send me her story "Gypsy Girl." I found this to be a very current piece of work, in terms of both style and content. The story reminds us of several recent high profile cases in which young people showed great courage in abusive situations. Lonning's crafty use of the "gypsy girl rules" to structure the narrative is not only hip—it's very effective. This tightly written story reminds us that we always have choices and opportunities—the trick is to act when the time is right.

Another protagonist who refuses to be limited is Thomas, in "One Extra Parking Space." He shows us that everyone can be proud of who they are, even someone "who will never in his lifetime be able to make change." Thomas reminds us that some human qualities, such as intelligence, can be used to separate one person from another, but that there are also qualities, such as wisdom and compassion, that reach across artificial divides, to build and maintain connection.

I wrote my contribution to this anthology, "The Frontiers of Knowledge," because someone just like Timothy took part in a workshop I gave to high school students in England. This young man talked about nothing but computers and his clever father, and clearly had nothing but contempt for women. Indeed, I had to get pretty tough with him before he would listen to what I had to say or treat the girls in our group with respect. It was only later, from his writing, that I came to understand the sadness peering out through those clunky mad-scientist glasses. This boy's airs and graces, like Timothy's, were nothing but show. The more he was hurt, the pricklier he became, and so he traveled through life, snarling at those he longed to touch.

"The Kind of Light That Shines on Texas," by Reginald McKnight, shows how three African American students are marginalized by the racism inherent in their recently integrated Texas high school. All three evolve radically different ways to survive. Ah-so retreats into sullen silence. Marvin does that odd thing with his arm, as if deliberately living down to negative stereotyping. Clint, McKnight's protagonist, tries to fit in—laughing along with the jokes and vying to be an "eraser duster." Though you'll be carried along by the action in this story, particularly the memorable fight scenes with the terrifying Oakley, I invite you to look for some of its subtleties. Pay close attention to Wickham, who manages to be almost seamlessly racist. Ask some tough questions: Do you feel any sympathy for Oakley? Is Clint a blameless hero? Who really wins the fight at the end? I've read this story several times, and I'm still struggling with these questions.

I received quite a few stories with gay protagonists. In some ways, "Playing the Garden," by Chris Fisher, might seem an unusual choice. After all, we never actually meet Kevin, whose coming-out is a catalyst for the events described in the piece. I liked this unusual point of view, however. It works perfectly to show the impact upon one family of society's sad insistence that there is only one acceptable way to love. Above all, it's never preachy or judgmental. "I can't understand," says the narrator in the first line, "the way some people's heads work." This story tries to bring understanding by honoring the varied and often conflicting views of its characters.

Another unusual choice, perhaps, is "Nobody Listens When I Talk" by Annette Sanford—a quiet story in which nothing, really, happens. For me, that was the whole point. "When you aren't really you, then the who that you are is different somehow: strong and part of everything," Marilyn, the teen narrator, points out. Perhaps we all need to spend some time like her, adrift in a porch swing. Sometimes the adult world makes just too many demands on young people, planning ways to fill up every moment of every day, forgetting that sometimes all you need to do is to drift, to dream, to take a holiday from being who you are.

Whether you're working to become a caring daughter or son, a loyal friend, a talented athlete, a musician, writer, or artist; whether you're applying to college, thinking about a career, taking care of someone who's sad or sick; whether you're fighting to establish your independence, to live up to someone else's expectations, or just to find out who you are and where you fit in, I hope this collection will give you the chance to curl up in a hammock, at least metaphorically speaking. I hope that you'll take time out to let life slip by while you take stock and regroup. Above all, I hope these stories will convince you that there are many different kinds of people in the world and also help you to treat them, and yourself, with compassion and kindness.

—CLAIRE ROBSON

# OUTSIDE RULES

# A Minstrel Visits

SANDELL MORSE

Every Christmas my mother brings home a weirdo. She's very big with the arts in Starkboro, New Hampshire. That's like being a hot shot ski racer in Florida. No mountains in Florida, no arts up here, except for this group she formed called Friends. They meet at the college. That's where she takes ballet. I used to take lessons, too, but not anymore. How would you like to be short and dumpy and have a mother who looks like all the blondes on TV?

"Susan," my mother says, rattling the doorknob. "Susan, unlock this door."

"It *is* unlocked." I don't tell her I've pushed a carton of books in front of it, and that's why it makes a scraping sound when she opens it.

"What in the world?" She stands in the doorway, hands on her hips. She's wearing black wool slacks and a sweater that glitters. She's piled her blonde hair on top of her head, except for a single strand that curls at her right temple.

"I'm packing stuff away. You're always telling me to clean up." She looks at the carton, then at me. I shrug and flop onto my bed. Hard. The headboard squeaks, and her eyebrows arch. I fold my arms under my head and stare at the ceiling. She doesn't want to start a fight. We don't have time. But, my room's a mess—clothes in piles on my rug, opened drawers spilling clothes, underpants hanging from a lamp shade, jars of creams with the tops left off, books and papers heaped on my desk, wet towels on a wooden chair, one with spindles up the back. My snow boots sit in front of the radiator, oozing mud. And on the floor next to my bed, a half-eaten box of chocolate chip cookies. I reach down, take a cookie, and nibble the edges. She eyes the box. She's on a new kick about my weight. Silence. Probably read about it in her book: *Surviving Your Daughter's Adolescence.* Fine with me.

"Susan," she says, "Peter Anthony's due any minute."

"So?" I pop the circle of cookie into my mouth and lick my fingers. "He's not sleeping here." Peter Anthony's one of her theater guys. They give classes and perform at the college. My mother invites them over, sometimes, for dinner and, later, for a whole week. My father says he doesn't mind. I don't get it.

She lifts a hand to the back of her neck. It's what she does whenever she's nervous or upset. "Susan," she says. "This room's an embarrassment."

"It's mine. What difference does it make?"

"Susan, you know I don't have time for this."

"Neither do I."

"I mean it."

"Mean what?"

She's quiet now because she knows we can go on like this. Forever. She walks to a window and looks out.

Our house is on a country road. Not many cars go by, so when we hear the sound of one, we listen. All I hear are winter sounds—ice melting and dripping from the roof, a branch cracking, a few dried leaves left on the oak tree, rustling, now, in the wind. If it weren't for my mother, I'd enjoy lying here on my bed, listening and thinking about Allison, the most popular girl in my class, who's almost my friend. Outside, a car climbs the hill, slows, and pulls into our driveway.

My mother turns. "Susan," she says, "why do you do this to me?"

I swing my legs and push up into a shoulder stand. "Do what?" I say in that tone she hates.

"We'll discuss this later," my mother says.

She leaves my room, and I count her footsteps, first in the hall, then on the stairs. When she reaches the bottom, I run to the window and peer out. Peter Anthony drives a yellow Volkswagen bug that now sits in our snow-filled driveway like a lost buttercup. He's a small man, sort of fat, and he's wearing a dark-colored knitted sweater with white reindeer prancing across his chest. He looks more like a troll than any dancer I've seen. The trumpet player who stayed with us last year had a pointy nose and furtive eyes like a fox, and the guy before that, the one who did the pantomimes, was short and bumpy like a frog. My mother thinks they're all handsome. Once, I tried to tell my father how she flirts with these guys. He laughed. "It doesn't mean a thing, Susan," he said to me. I felt dumb, not the kind of dumb you feel when you don't know an answer in school, the kind of dumb you feel when a grownup makes you into a little kid.

Downstairs, I push open the swinging door that separates the dining room from the kitchen. My mother's standing at the counter near the sink, boning a chicken breast. "Oh, Susan," she says, "you're here."

Duh, I want to say.

Peter Anthony extends his hand. "How nice to see you." His fingers are warm.

"Susan," my mother says, pointing with her knife, "we'll need a salad. There's lettuce in the refrigerator." Then, to Peter Anthony, "Now where were we? Paris, wasn't it? This year or last?" Her voice goes soft. "I envy you, Peter. All your exciting travel."

"And I envy this," Peter Anthony says. He sweeps the kitchen with his hand, then leans back against the table. "The last time I was here—well, not right here, not in your lovely home, but at the college—I don't remember your telling me you were dancer."

I stuff lettuce into a spinner and turn the handle on top, leaning all of my weight into the job. If I make enough noise maybe I can drown her out. I know what's coming. It's the old "I was a dancer in New York" story. That's where she met my father.

Peter Anthony eyes my mother—her waist, her hips. "Ah," he says, "I should have known. The way you moved in class that day. Training."

I stop the spinner, lift the top, and rip the lettuce into tiny pieces. She hates tiny pieces. My mother sighs. "I can't believe it still shows. So many years here in this wilderness." Her voice trails off.

She's lying. Showing off. She likes it here, mostly.

"Those are things we never lose," Peter Anthony says. He steps to the center of the kitchen, draws his feet into fifth position, does a *plié*, and turns on his toes. When he stops, he's facing me. He winks and turns again. Turns are something I never learned. I used to hop around instead of spin. Peter has done a triple. "Do you dance, Susan?" he says to me.

I mumble, "Used to."

"She could have been good," my mother says.

I glare, remembering the way she picked on me—lift your chin, suck in your gut, tuck your fanny. She wanted me to look like her. I wanted to, too. Not that I'd tell *her* that. I'm short and square like my father. And I have a bubble butt.

Peter Anthony takes my hand, bows, and kisses my fingers. Still holding on, he lifts my arm. I turn under it. "Come with me." Dancing, he leads me outside to his car.

It's cold, but I don't mind. Up close, the yellow Volkswagen reminds me of my room, the way it spills over with stuff— pots and dishes, clothes and linens, records and tapes, a standing lamp, even a small television set. I blow air through my lips and whistle. "Don't you have a house?"

"I'm like a snail. I carry it all on my back." He hands me a box. "My kitchen."

I wonder if he's teasing me. But then again, I think maybe he's not.

"In olden days they called us minstrels. We sang for our supper. Now we work at colleges and people like your mother take us in."

I look at him from under my brow. "My mother?"

"It's not so bad. I meet the nicest people this way."

In the kitchen, Peter Anthony lifts a bottle of olive oil out of his box and sets it on our wooden table. I read labels— mustard pickle, tomato jam, peach chutney. I sniff spice jars and smell smells I've never smelled, turmeric, cardamom. "If you don't mind," Peter Anthony says to my mother, "I'm an expert with oil and vinegar. A few spices."

"How nice," my mother says. She opens a jar of Peter's tiny pickled onions, pops one into her mouth, and chews slowly.

I want to gag. "Think I'll watch some TV."

"Not so fast," Peter Anthony says, grabbing my wrist. "I need you to mash the garlic." He pulls a small marble bowl from his kitchen box and hands me a matching marble stick. Then, he peels a clove of garlic and drops it in. "Mash it against the sides. Mortar and pestle. It's the only proper way."

My mother slips a metal garlic press into a kitchen drawer, but not before I catch her. Peter Anthony sees her, too. I bring the marble stick down onto the garlic clove. It slides away. I hit it, again. This time, it pops up and out of the bowl. I put it back. I try again. Finally, I kind of slide the marble stick down the side of the bowl and sneak up on the clove. I mash, slowly. "Is this good enough?" I want to know.

"A little more," Peter says. When I finish, he adds mustard, vinegar, olive oil, and spices. "Drop in a pinch of sugar, Susan."

"Me?"

"You." He hands me the sugar bowl. I add sugar. "Now, taste," he says. I eye my mother, then stick my pinky into the mixture. "What do you think?" he says to me.

"It's good," I say, offering the marble bowl.

He pours the dressing over the lettuce. I can't believe it. My mother checks every little thing I do, and I can see from the curve of her back that she's annoyed.

The phone rings. It's my father, calling to say he'll be late, and Peter Anthony has already poured the dressing onto the salad. He shrugs, then smiles at me.

On Christmas morning, we open Peter's gifts—family games of Stockmarket, Monopoly, and Chinese Checkers. He's brought a silk scarf for my mother, a tie for my father, and a glass unicorn for me. My mother tells me it's blown glass. I hold it in my palm. The lights of the Christmas tree pulse, and my unicorn has a heart. No one else sees it beat. We have given Peter Anthony a red wool scarf that I wind around his neck. I step back. He acts pleased. It's obvious, though, his gifts are more generous than ours.

"Peter, you shouldn't have," my mother says.

"Don't let her kid you," my father says. "She loves every minute of it." He has given her gold earrings with tiny diamonds that she picked out herself weeks before. She kisses his forehead, then his lips. How embarrassing. She's wearing a velour robe that zips up the front, and her long hair is pulled back and tied with a bow. A curl of red ribbon sticks to the toe of her black velvet slipper. My father pats her on the butt. A buzzer sounds in the kitchen, and I jump up. "I'll get it."

Walking, now, to the kitchen, I can feel it, the fat in my behind, wiggling and jiggling. I won't tell her, but I promise myself, I'll lose weight. I turn off the buzzer and pull a cinnamon cake from the oven. When it's cool enough, I pick the pecans from the top and pop them into my mouth. Then, I sift confectioner's sugar over the indentations.

In the living room, my mother's eyes scan the cake. Wordlessly, she slices wedges, then slides each wedge onto a plate. They're fancy plates, bone china, she bought at an auction with my father. She pours coffee. My father is talking to Peter Anthony, asking him about places he's been— England, Australia, New Zealand, Hawaii. "One day," my father says, "but you know how it is. If it's not a piece of machinery breaking down, it's a problem with one of the shifts." He owns a plant that makes crutches, wooden ones.

"Excuses," my mother says. "The truth is he's happy here," she says to Peter.

It's one of their arguments. He never wants to go anywhere; she does.

"I guess she told you I whisked her away from the glamorous life," my father says.

I help myself to a second slice of coffee cake and talk around the food in my mouth. "I thought you were just trying out for the chorus," I say.

"The *corps de ballet*," my mother says. Her voice is icy.

"Same difference."

My father throws me a look as if to tell me I've said enough. He pushes himself out of his chair. "What do you say we hunt up the snowshoes and hike up to Patterson's Pond?"

Like he doesn't know where they are.

Peter laughs. "You actually own snowshoes?"

"And cross-country skis. And downhill skis," my father says. "But for a novice . . ."

Peter interrupts. "Not for me. I'm comfortable right here."

"Me too." The truth is, exercise makes me sick. I see the nurse whenever it's time for gym.

"Please, join us, Peter," my mother says.

"Leave him be," my father says to my mother. "Susan's here." Then to me, "Maybe, you'll play one of those games."

"Maybe," I say.

"Come on, Martha," my father says.

We stand at the door, watching them leave, two figures lifting their knees and walking side by side past the garage and into the woods. I turn on the TV, then settle into the soft cushions of the couch. Peter Anthony sits in my father's reclining chair and tilts back. My unicorn stands on a low table where the lights of the Christmas tree make rainbows in its spiral horn. We're waiting for the *The Nutcracker* to come on. Peter used to be in it, not this version, but another one, a long time ago, he says. In the meantime, Baryshnikov dances a commercial, and I ask Peter if he can leap and jump like that.

"Never," he says.

I giggle.

"Do you remember the old woman? The one with all the children?"

One year when my mother took me Boston to see *The Nutcracker,* see it live instead of on TV, I saw a woman wearing a giant skirt that looked like a curtain. Children ran out from under it. The old woman reached. She pulled them back. She missed. She tried again. It was the funniest scene.

"I used to play that role," Peter says.

I give him one of my looks. "Come on."

"You could say I'm more of an actor than a dancer. A stunt man." He smiles. "Of sorts."

"So you jumped off cliffs and hung from ladders?"

"Not exactly. Come. I'll show you."

In the front hall, he climbs the stairs. I start to follow, but he tells me to wait. I lean back against the big wooden door, a door we never use. Outside, an orange snowplow rumbles past. Peter Anthony calls, "Ready?"

Before I can answer, Peter is falling, rolling down the flight of stairs and landing at my feet. I can't believe he isn't hurt. He stands and grips my shoulders. "All you do is roll. Shoulder to shoulder. Give it a try."

"Are you kidding?"

"Trust me."

I lie in the middle of the staircase, my body tucked into a ball as Peter lowers me from step to step. "It's like a sideways somersault, but you'll have to practice."

The next three days, whenever my mother leaves the house, I roll myself down the stairs, slowly at first, then faster. One afternoon, Peter teaches me to stage-fight. "It's like a dance," he says, moving toward me. He claps his hands. I clap, and he snaps his head so sharply, I almost believe I've slapped him. We clap; we grunt; we scream. I'm sweating now, moving in close when Peter falls to the floor and rolls from side to side, moaning. He lies on his back, eyes closed. He's very still. I kneel and put my ear to his chest. "Peter, Peter, wake up." I hold my breath. A heart thumps, but I don't know whose. Mine or his? I whisper his name. When he doesn't answer, I dig my ear into his sweater. It's his heart. I know it is. "Peter, if you're fooling me, I'll never speak to you again."

He bolts up. "Gotcha."

I punch his stomach, but not too hard, and run around the dining room table. He's at one end, and I'm at the other. We're holding the backs of chairs, swaying from side to side. I let go and run smack into Peter's chest. "Let's see what you've learned," he says.

We're in the living room now, slapping and falling when my mother walks in and says my name. We stop. It's like that game of human statues. She gives us a look that could kill. "What's going on?" she wants to know.

I mumble. "Nothing."

"It doesn't look like nothing to me."

I blow out my breath. "Stage-fighting. Peter taught me."

"Her timing is excellent," Peter says. "She gets that from you, I'm sure." He smiles, then claps his hand beside my cheek.

My mother is not pleased. "That's enough, Susan." Her hand is at the back of her neck, brushing at strands of loose hair.

"Why? What's wrong?"

She eyes me. "We can talk about this later."

"No. I want to talk now."

"I said later, Susan."

I push past her and stomp up the stairs, listening to every sound I make. I slam my bedroom door, but I'm not inside, I'm sneaking down the hallway to listen when I hear words—"stage-fighting," "no harm," "lovely child." Peter is saying them.

My mother's voice: "daughter." I climb down to the middle of the stairs. "And frankly, Peter, " my mother says, "it doesn't look right, the two of you wrestling on the rug like that."

"Martha. . . . " Peter says. He doesn't say anything more.

In my room, I remember the warm rough wool of Peter's sweater. I remember his heart, thumping and beating under my ear.

Late that night, I walk barefoot on the wooden floorboards and knock softly on Peter's door. A nightlight dimly burns in the hall. The house is quiet and smooth around me. I hold my mouth close to the place where door and frame meet. "Peter, it's me, Susan."

He opens the door, and I step inside. Before it closes, he props the door, holding it open with a shoe. It's late, but he's still dressed, wearing trousers, a shirt, and his reindeer sweater. "I was sitting up reading," he says to me, but I see his opened suitcase.

"Are you leaving?"

"In the morning."

I hug his waist and hold on.

"Susan," he says.

"I don't want you to go. You didn't do anything. It's her. She gets that way."

"Susan, she's concerned about you. If I had a daughter, I'd be concerned, too."

"Why? We didn't do anything wrong. I heard you say so. She wants me to be like her, and I'm not. Even my father thinks she's perfect."

He pries my fingers from his waist and holds my hands. I jerk free, then I reach into the pocket of my nightgown. It's where I've put my unicorn. It stands, now, on my flattened palm, mane curling, front legs prancing. I look through its crystal body and see Peter's fingers reaching for mine. He takes the unicorn and drops it back into my pocket. He holds the tips of my fingers and reads the lines in my palm. "First, I see sadness. Maybe tears. Then, great happiness. A trip."

I stare and imagine myself in Peter's little yellow car. Peter is driving, left arm bent, elbow resting on the opened window frame, fingers steadying the wheel. We're traveling across a vast desert. Sand swirls up from the tires and pings the doors. A hot wind blows and lifts my hair. We're in California, heading west toward the ocean. My unicorn hangs from the rear view mirror, rays of sun shining through and dropping crystal triangles into my lap.

My mother stands in the doorway. I don't know how long she's been there, and I don't care. I pull my hand from Peter's hand and push past her. I flick on the lights in the hall, then hurl myself down the stairs. My head is tucked, and my shoulders roll as if on a cushion of air.

"Susan," she shrieks.

I land in a heap and watch her black velvet slippers through half-closed eyes. She descends the stairs and kneels beside me. She whispers my name. Giggles bump inside my stomach. They bubble up; I swallow them down. In the living room, the clock on the mantle chimes the hour. My mother's hand reaches out. I'm waiting, waiting for her to touch my shoulder before I laugh.

# Mr. Softee

WALLY LAMB

School's been out less than a week and my parents are already driving me crazy. "Mow the lawn! Vacuum out the pool! Read the newspaper!" The last suggestion seems like the easiest, so I pick up the want ads section to make them happy. That's where the trouble begins. Mr. Softee needs licensed drivers for summer ice cream routes. "Earn up to $150 per wk. Must be 17 yrs of age, neat, dependable. Reliable driving record a must."

What I'm picturing driving over to the interview is one heck of a summer: cool breezes floating in through the sliding window of my ice cream truck and me wearing one of those shiny Hawaiian shirts with the pineapples and little Hawaiian guys surfing all over it. Kids'll love me and so will their big-spender parents. Best of all, these twenty or so gorgeous babes will be lining up regularly for a cone and a minute's worth of my time. The whole picture's getting me so excited that I just miss bashing into the back of a Toyota, nearly wiping out my "reliable driving record."

And I do get the job. Only being Mr. Softee isn't exactly the way I had pictured it. They make you wear this white uniform and a goofy-looking paper hat that says "Have a Nice Day" on it. Since I'm low man, I get this truck with a busted door that I have to keep closed with a rope. On top of that, my route is in this section of town called The Flats.

The Flats is one of those neighborhoods where there's an abandoned grocery store cart about every ten feet. Little six-year-old kids are running around with dried snot mustaches saying junk like "I hate your guts," and worse. The whole project is lousy with noise: soap operas blaring away, some guy yelling at his wife, and these scrawny junior high girls blasting scratchy forty-fives on those cheap little plastic record players.

My first day driving over there, I'm moaning to myself that with all these poor people for customers, I'm liable to break the world record for low pay. Only I see I'm wrong by about the third minute. People hear these idiotic bells we've got on the truck and come running like I'm the pope or something. And I'm in the land of big spenders, too—no lie. This fat guy orders a Strawberry Royale—one of our buck-and-a-half numbers—and it's not even ten-thirty in the morning. The lady behind him wants chocolate shakes for herself and each of her three slimy kids. I'm thinking to myself, This isn't going to be so bad after all. That's when I see this vision that looks like she's just floated off one of those Coppertone billboards. And she's coming right over to the truck.

"Could I get you something, miss?" She's wearing cutoffs and this white bathing suit top looking good enough to make a tough guy like Clint Eastwood start crying. I'm smiling like I got a comb stuck sideways in my mouth, but I figure I'm not being fake—just charming.

"Well, I am kind of thirsty," she says, "but my money's in the house. So you make cherry Cokes like the last guy? I love cherry Cokes."

"It just so happens I do have the secret recipe—ha ha."

Her face goes blank on me.

"But . . . uh . . . why don't I make a sample and you can test it for me—free of charge. I need the practice. You'd be doing me the favor."

She picks up on this offer, I tell you. So I whip up this complicated "recipe" for her—two squirts of cherry syrup in a Coke and stir. I shove open the window and hand the goddess her soda. Man, she's even got sexy hands. That's when this weasel-faced younger girl who's about as skinny as a Q-tip comes up to the window and breaks the spell.

"Gimme a lime dip top with chocolate ice cream and red sprinkles," she says. She's squinting behind these turquoise cat's-eye glasses.

"Large or small, Racquel?" I ask the squirt. The goddess lets out this laugh that sounds like high keys on a piano make.

"My name ain't Racquel, it's Debbie. And if you make fun of me, I'll have my mother call up and say you're flirting with girls and giving 'em free stuff. Large. With extra sprinkles."

I hand Debbie her cone—it's all I can do not to barf making it—and she pays me.

"Charlene's got a new one, Charlene's got a new one," she starts chanting as she struts away from the truck. There's red sprinkles all over her lips and she's twitching her butt like someone plugged her in.

At that moment I might have seen Charlene lift up her arm and sort of shoot Debbie this gesture you wouldn't exactly do in front of your grandmother. And then again, I might not have either. I didn't see it that clearly, so she probably didn't even do it.

"So how's the Coke?"

"You put more cherry in yours. It's different . . . pretty good."

"Thanks. So your name's Charlene or what?" I ask, kind of nonchalantly wiping down the equipment, trying not to show her she's giving me the shakes.

"Yeah," she says.

We strike up a little chitchat. I tell her I'm going to be a senior at Alumni. She says she's a junior at Tech, studying something called Beauty Culture. All I can picture is this mold I grew in a Petri dish in biology lab last year. Not that I wanted to. They made us.

"You sort of look like Derek on *All My Children*," she says.

"Oh yeah?" I tell her, flashing my comb smile all over the place. "So look, my name's Eli."

"Eel eye?" she says kind of put off. "Oh wow, gross."

"No, no. Eli. E-L-I." She's not exactly Scholar of the Year, that much I can tell.

"I never heard of that name," she says like she doesn't care much one way or the other. "Well, see you." She drops her cup in the middle of the street and strolls back toward her house, treating me to the way she looks from the back. I practically fall right through the window.

Yes sir, things are looking up for old Mr. Softee. Only there's something sort of weird going on. All the time we've been talking, I keep getting the feeling someone's watching us. On the off chance it's my boss in an unmarked car, I throw seventy-five cents of my own money in the cash box to cover the cherry Coke. Stupid, I know.

For the next couple of weeks, things are so-so. I'm raking in the dough for sure, but Charlene's running hot and cold. One day she's super friendly, and the next day it's like she's forgotten I've given her about three thousand dollars' worth of free merchandise. (I've begun to throw dollar bills into the cash box by now, but I tell myself it's like one of my father's investments.)

And all this time this is going on, I keep getting the feeling someone's watching. Only I'm not sure. I figure it might even be my own conscience staring at me. Only what have I done to feel guilty about? It's a Friday. We're in the middle of this heat wave that won't quit. The weather lady's predicting we'll hit one hundred degrees for the third straight day. On top of that, the generator that runs my freezer is on the blink. With every stop I make, the ice cream looks more pathetic. Instead of swirling up into peaks as it comes out of the machine, it's sort of lying over on its side.

When I get to Charlene's apartment house, I park my truck in the usual spot, but she's nowhere around. That's when this little mystery I've been wondering about gets solved. The hairy eyeball I've been picking up on my radar comes off this shabby porch in full view.

And what a sight! She's dressed in this flowery blouse thing with a ton of ruffles and those designer jeans no girl sixty or seventy pounds overweight ought to be wearing. She's got this hair that's some freaked-out cross between Shirley Temple and the Bride of Frankenstein and she's wearing about a hundred pounds of noisy jewelry. Just seeing her makes the day ten degrees hotter.

"Oh, hello," she says in this phony surprised voice, like I just drove onto her porch instead of her getting up and waddling over to my window.

"Yo," I say. "Get you something?"

"Are you the new driver for the neighborhood?"

"Yup. What'll you have?"

"Umm . . . let me think . . . a small pineapple sundae."

"Look, my freezer's kind of on strike. It's going to be sort of soupy."

"Well, how about a root beer float, then? That way, soupy ice cream doesn't even matter." She pops me this little kewpie doll dimple and shifts her weight so's I hear her jewelry clacking. Man, she's sweating like a pig.

"Suit yourself." I shrug and go to town on her float.

"This truck is cute inside."

"Yeah? . . . Oh, well, thanks."

It's a good thing I've got my back to her. My eyes are rolling like a slot machine. "Here's your float. Ninety-five."

She passes a dollar bill back to me. Her fingers look like little sausages and there're these cheap rings on every one of them. I give her change and she just stands there, like our business transaction hasn't been completed. She's sipping away and smiling at me so's I'm getting the creeps.

"Do you mind if I give you some advice?" she finally says. She wrinkles her nose cutesy-style. I'm practically barfing.

"Funny, I don't remember writing to Dear Abby," I tell her. On a hundred-degree day, the last thing I need is this loser telling me I don't put enough ice cream in my floats. She shoots me a look like I harpooned her. "Okay, what? What's the advice?"

"Well, don't get mad, but I think you should stay away from Charlene Avery. You seem like a nice guy and she just uses people. Guys especially. I think you'll just get hurt. She bleaches her hair, even the hair on her arms. That's sick."

My mouth drops open like a glove compartment.

"Well, you don't have to look like you're going to kill me. I'm just telling you for your own good."

"Look, whatever your name is, don't worry about it. I can take care of myself." Only it comes out unconvincing, like I'm John-Boy Walton.

"I'm telling you, she's a regular piranha fish with guys. Believe me, I've known her since fourth grade!"

I spot skinny Debbie running toward the truck, and would you believe I'm actually glad to see her? Dear Abby is so hopped up, she's gotten to the end of her float and doesn't realize it. She's making that dry slurpy sound you make when all a straw is doing is sucking up dead air.

"Hi, Debbie," she says, cautious-like, as if she's afraid of the squirt.

"Oh, hi Doris. Would you stand back? I haven't gotten my cootie shot today." She starts spraying the air with this imaginary aerosol can.

I wait on Debbie and then on two other customers. By this time Doris seems to have disappeared, which is fine with me. Then my faithful generator starts dying out on me again, and when I get back into the truck, there she is, leaning against the back, playing with her straw.

"Look out, will you? I gotta get outta here."

"She hates my guts because of the time I almost got her arrested."

"What? Who?"

"Charlene! She was babysitting last summer and her and this stupid boyfriend of hers named Kenny were jeopardizing the baby. So I called up the cops and reported them. It's sort of a hobby of mine."

"Calling the cops?"

"No, defending poor, defenseless people who can't help themselves. I'm like the kid in that book *Catcher in the Rye*. Did you ever read it?"

Did I ever read it! It's only in my top five out of the best books I ever read in my whole life. "Nope," I tell her from up in the machinery, "never heard of it. I try not to read books if I can help it."

"That's weird," she says, "because I know you had Mrs. Allen for junior English this past year and she said she did that book with all her junior classes. She recommended it to me. Anyway, this main character named Holden always wants to help out poor, defenseless people, except he's a real basket case about it. For me it's more like a hobby."

"You go to Alumni?"

"I'm going into sophomore year." Man, she's only a kid and she already looks like someone's bimbo aunt.

"Yeah, well, I'm a senior there."

"I know. Mrs. Allen said you were a good writer. She let

me read that poem you wrote called 'Identity,' with the guy walking along the beach by himself, trying to decide who he really was. It was so-ooo good. I even copied it down on the back cover of my notebook. It's in the house. You want to see?"

"That's okay, I already read it," I tell her.

"So that's how I recognized you the first day you started here. I'm glad you replaced that other guy. He always gypped you on large cones. Now, he's someone who almost deserved Charlene."

"So why do you think I'm helpless and need someone to protect me?"

"You aren't a Capricorn, are you? Capricorns have a basic mistrust of those who are their true friends. I don't think you're totally helpless. You just need help with dangerous girls like Charlene. It's because you're so sensitive. Which is why I thought you were a Libra."

The fact that I am a Libra is just a lucky shot. What a whole lot of junk that is.

"So what did Charlene do to this baby that you called the cops for?" By this time the generator's going again and I'm walking around to make it sound like I don't care if she answers or not.

"Well, it was her boyfriend, Kenny, more than her. But she was watching him and laughing. You see that house— the gray one three down? This lady, Mrs. Kudlak, lives up on the third floor. She's the one Charlene used to sit for."

I look up at this dilapidated ark of a place. The top floor has one of those walk-on porches with the curtains sticking outside because there aren't any screens or anything.

"This guy Kenny had the baby out on the porch. You know how people throw babies up in the air and catch them to make them laugh?"

"You called the cops because he was playing with a baby?"

"Well, yeah. Because he was holding her over the porch railing and doing it there. The baby was laughing and squealing, having a great time, but can you just imagine?"

I look over at the building again and picture this baby in mid-fall. My stomach does one of those numbers like I'm on the express elevator riding down. "So what happened then?" I say. "Mrs. Whatchacallit fires Charlene and you get yourself a new babysitting job, right?"

"No way. No one around here will hire me to babysit because they think I'm weird. Which is totally stupid, because I understand kids very well and can relate to them, not like some people I know who bleach their arm hair. Mrs. Kudlak found out it was me that called the cops, and she came over and swore at my mother. She fired Charlene, though. That's when Charlene started telling everyone I have bugs."

In a way, I feel sort of sorry for her. She didn't call the cops to be mean or anything. "Hey, look, I've got to get going. I'm already running late."

"Okay, Au revoir. And you make delicious root beer floats," she says, flopping back across the street, giving me a rear-view shot that makes her look pretty wicked hopeless.

"Hey, Doris," I yell.

She looks around, sort of surprised.

"Is Charlene still going out with that Kenny guy?"

She shakes her head like she's real disgusted or hurt or something.

If I hurt her, she sure gets over it in a hurry. All the next week, I can't even take the right onto her street before she's galloping off her porch like one of those Clydesdale horses in the beer ads. Every day I'm scanning the horizon for Charlene the Queen, who's doing this extended disappearing act, and pesty Doris is buzzing around me like a three-hundred-pound mosquito, asking me all these dopey questions, like do I believe in reincarnation and who do I think are the worst teachers at our school and what albums do I have? Not only that, but she's giving me all her own answers to these questions, like I almost care to hear them.

Only, what am I supposed to do? She's a paying customer—Miss Root Beer Float of the year, which is what she orders every single day after the first one. I mean, she's pretty predictable for a weirdo.

"Mmm, you keep making these better and better, Eli. What's your favorite flower?"

"What do you mean, what's my favorite flower? What's your favorite size wrench? I don't have a favorite flower."

"Relax. It's only because I'm making this flower collage for one of my girlfriends for her birthday and I want to have everyone who she likes' favorite flower on it. She knows who you are from school and thinks you're cute and not conceited like your friends."

"Oh yeah? What's she look like?" It's starting to dawn on me that these girlfriends she brings up all the time are about as real as the Stairway to Heaven.

"Making collages is another one of my hobbies. I have eight hobbies, counting helping people. I collect dogs and I draw. Sometimes I write stories . . . "

"That's terrific," I say in this real bored voice, "but if you'll excuse me, J. D. Salinger, someone's trying to buy an ice cream."

"How'd you know who he was if you never read *Catcher in the Rye*?"

I give my customer his Cho-Cho Bar, and he shoots Doris this look like she's got two heads. She doesn't even seem to notice.

"So, think! You must have some flower you at least kind of like."

"Okay, okay, roses. My favorite flower is roses." I get tired of playing Twenty Questions, so I pepper back one of my own that's sure to make Doris turn and run.

"So listen, where's Charlene been hiding herself these days?"

There's this long pause. Then she says, real huffy, "What I'd like to know, Eli, is why you even care. Would you pick up poison and drink it?"

"Only if it looked like Charlene."

Then—this kills me—she puts her big puss against the side of the truck and starts sobbing, Hollywood-style. "I didn't want to hurt you," she says when she finally looks up, all bleary eyed. "But since you want to know, Charlene's been going out with this divorced guy, Ted, who's got tattoos that say gross things on them. So there!" She lifts her chin up and waddles across the street like she's Queen Elizabeth, afraid of dropping her crown.

I figure this guy Ted is about as real as Doris' girl-friends, but just the same, I can see him and Charlene yucking it up at the beach or something and it makes me real mad. Real mad!

I call in sick the next day. And I am sick in a way: sick of waiting around for Charlene to show, sick of The Flats and all the losers who live there. Only taking the day off does-n't cure a thing.

Wednesday, July 23, is the kind of day it would be worth jumping down a flight of concrete stairs head-first for just so's you could get amnesia and forget you lived through it.

Doris' radar is better than ever. As soon as I turn onto her street, she comes bombing out of her house with this big sheet of cardboard in her hand.

"Where were you yesterday?" she demands. "I wanted to give you something. I was worried about you."

"Don't I have a right to one crummy sick day? You're a customer, Doris. You don't have any right to worry about me."

"So sorry, Mr. Touchy. I'd like a root beer float, please," she says handing me this sweaty stack of change. I make her the float, thinking maybe it's time to lower the boom. That's when I notice she's done something different with her hair—don't ask me what—and she's wearing this rose in it, just above the ear. Only this isn't a long-stemmed beauty from the florist. It's a scraggly bug-eaten orange thing. She's probably even stuck the thorn into her head to keep it on just to prove how much she loves me.

"What I wanted to give you was this. It's a surprise—a combination friendship and apology present. I hope you like it. And I'm sorry I got mad just because you asked one dense question about Charlene. She's not even worth fighting over."

She stuffs this poster thing through the window, wearing a look like I'm about to announce the million-dollar lottery winner. I can tell she's got the shakes, because that little rose is actually vibrating, no lie. What she's gone and done is copied my poem, "Identity," down in this sickening curlicue writing and illustrated it with this guy walking on a beach. As if that's not enough, she's made this border around the whole thing by cutting pictures of roses out of magazines and liquor ads and stuff.

The guy on the beach is supposed to be me, I guess, only he's got this kind of hunchback and a puffy hairdo like one of those men dolls they sell in toy departments. And the ocean's got these little loops for waves, like maybe a second-grader would draw. It's a real F-minus job from start to finish, but it gets to me all the same, so's I have to turn away and start scrubbing the hell out of the sauce dispensers.

"Geez, thanks, Doris. I appreciate it, only . . ."

"I knew you'd like it because you're so sensitive. It took me seventeen hours to finish, but a lot of that time I was just looking for roses. I couldn't get enough, so I had to go to that store Garden of Eden in the mall and buy a seed catalog. They charged me two dollars for the stupid thing, but at least there were plenty of roses in it. So it was a surprise? D'you like it?"

"Yeah, sure. It's really great."

"That's your poem, you know. I copied it from my notebook. Recognize it?"

"Uh huh . . . I like the lettering."

"So where do you think you'll put it? I sort of made it for your bedroom if that's where you want to hang it up. Would it go there okay—the colors?"

"Hey look, Doris, you know what? I still feel a little sick from yesterday with this heat and everything. Do you by any chance have two aspirin I could borrow?" I feel like I can't breathe with her there.

"I guess so. Hold on," she says and starts running back to her apartment.

"Slow down!" I yell to her. "It feels like it's in the nineties."

"Okay. Sorry, sir," she yells back in this voice that's so happy I want to bang my fist into something.

That's when I notice a screen door slam across the street and the long-lost Charlene sauntering over my way. She's wearing this low-cut tube top number that could send Bo Derek into early retirement.

"Hi gorgeous," the conversation begins. Only she's talking to me. "Long time no see."

So this is it. I've got to ask her out or I will self-destruct. Only out of the corner of my eye, Doris' corny poster is, like, looking at me.

"Hot day. Care for a cherry Coke?"

"Gimme a large vanilla cone instead. I'm starving," she says. I know she doesn't have any money stashed in that tube top of hers, but this is true love we're talking. I hand her the cone and notice this funny buzzed-out look in her eyes. She's so stoned it's a miracle she can even talk. She stands there giggling and scarfing down her large vanilla like it's going to save her life. She's dripping it all over herself, too, and thinking that's a scream. For some reason, even acting goofy like that, she looks older than before—older than me, even. Which is stupid, because she's a year behind me in school. I know this sounds ridiculous, but I almost feel afraid of her.

About this time, Doris comes flying out of her house and spots Charlene. She stands there a minute, getting her back up like a cat. Charlene's facing the truck and doesn't see a thing. Then Doris has this kind of tantrum. First she flings what looks like my two aspirin into the street. Then she goes back into her house, slamming the door so's I think her whole shabby building's going to cave in. Next thing you know, she comes creeping out again and slouches down on her porch like her body doesn't have any bones. And all the time, she's staring at me with these killer, laser-beam eyes.

Charlene's lapping up her cone, her eyes about as wide as traffic lights. "Hey, can I come inside and see what it looks like? Pleeeease?"

I start reciting the boss' rule about no one else in the truck with the driver and untying the stupid door at the same time.

"God, it looks so small from in here," Charlene says, licking her finger, then sticking it into the chocolate sprinkles and sucking them up. "What's this?"

"Seltzer water."

"What's this?"

"Hot fudge machine."

"Mmm. What's this?" she says, holding up Doris' poster.

"Oh . . . some stupid thing someone made for me . . . "

"Who? A girl? Someone from around here?"

"Well, yeah . . . I guess so . . . Doris Weigel."

"Lard ass made this?" She starts laughing and spraying the thing with that imaginary can of bug spray.

"She's actually quite clean," I sort of mumble.

Charlene starts reading my poem out loud. I can feel myself turning as red as the strawberry sauce.

"Yeah, I can't get rid of her. What a loser, huh?" I say. I almost feel stoned myself, having Charlene in the truck with me and it being so hot and everything.

"Hey, is this your name on the bottom? What is it—a poem?" Only she pronounces it "pome."

"What? Well, yeah, see . . . "

"Did you write this or something? I never knew guys wrote poetry."

"Well I didn't want to. It was for English. It's a long story."

"Poetry is so gay," she says. "Wait'll I see Doris. Man, that chick is so weird. Her whole family is. She's got this older brother who got arrested for making obscene phone calls. What a pervert! And her mother's a space case, too. She used to walk Doris back and forth to school every day until eighth grade."

"Where's her father?"

"She don't have one."

"So that explains it," I say, "they must have hatched her in a test tube."

Charlene loves this one, let me tell you. Then she drops the poster on the floor and goes charging into the cab. "Hey, let me drive this thing!"

That's when everything begins to kind of tip over and spill out.

"Well, what I'd like to know is if you want to go out this coming Saturday night after my shift, or maybe we could go to the beach on Monday on account of that's my day off."

"Well, what I'd like to know is if I can drive this truck before I give you an answer," she says, like we're playing Let's Make a Deal.

"Gee, I don't know, Charlene. We're not supposed to. Do you have your license?" I'm sort of whining.

"What do you think?" she asks me.

What I think is she doesn't, but the next thing you know, I'm giving her this crash-course lecture on shifting, which neither of us is listening to because she's slid her hands into the back pockets of my pants and is sorta, well, rubbing against me. Laser Eye Doris is probably burning a hole in the side of the truck by now, for sure.

I figure the sooner I get this over with, the better, so I release the parking brake and Charlene shifts into first gear, just like I tell her. She's giggling like crazy, but I'm thinking nothing can go wrong as long as I keep telling her exactly what to do. We begin inching down the street and everything's okay.

We pick up a little speed and all of a sudden, Charlene shifts right from first gear to third without me telling her to. The whole truck starts shaking.

"Put the clutch in! You're gonna stall. Step on the clutch!"

Only she guns the gas instead and we go sailing down the street.

"Hey cool it!" I'm yelling at her. "Chill out!" She's acting real strange, making these squealing tire noises. I go to grab the steering wheel away from her, but she pulls it hard to the left. We shoot across the road, hop the curb, and go careening toward this little kid in a diaper who's walking around throwing piles of dirt up in the air.

"Holy... whoaa," I remember screaming. I pull the steering wheel as hard as I can, and we take this sharp right just in time. We go flying across someone's lawn and back down onto the street. That's when I fall down on the floor, bringing Charlene with me. We do this crash landing right into a mailbox. Not exactly a pile-up at the Demolition Derby, but I'm scared as anything.

The little kid in the diaper starts bawling his head off.

"We coulda just wasted that little sucker!" I scream at Charlene. Man, I'm all shook up. "Get out of my truck, you . . . piranha!"

"Well, next time don't grab the wheel away from me!" she screams back. You could tell I had embarrassed her. "And by the way, forget about me going anywhere with you. I like real guys. You better stick with Doris Weigel." She unties the door, kicks it open with the heel of her bare foot, and storms off the truck. The she turns and shoots me the same X-rated gesture she gave Debbie—this time there isn't any mistaking it. I stand there tongue-tied. I can't even think of a good line to leave her with, although I thought of a couple of doozies the next day.

Doris comes flip-flopping down the street like no one's told her the emergency's over. She grabs the little squirt we've almost plowed into and starts squeezing him to death. He and Doris are both crying.

"You stupid jerk!" she almost screams at me, "You almost killed him! Get out! Get out of here! I hate your guts!"

Scrawny Debbie is up on the sidewalk, staring at me like I'm the weirdo. Next thing you know, I start crying, too. Can you believe it—a senior in high school? I guess it's the heat.

"I hate yours, too, you stupid fat goddamn loser!" Then I grab ahold of that poster, tear it up into five or six pieces, and send them sailing out the door of the truck. Backing up, I see the mailbox has this stupid little dent that's not even worth mentioning. I think I even lay rubber getting out of there. I drive a good mile and a half before I realize the bang, bang, banging I keep hearing isn't the blood pounding in my head but the door on the truck which I've forgotten to tie back up.

On the way back to the office that night, I decide the incident is so insignificant it's not even worth reporting.

Only when I park my truck, there's my boss waiting for me with my severance pay and the grand kiss-off.

"I can't have someone driving for me who's reckless around kids," she yells at me. "This is the first complaint I've ever received from the community."

Community, my left foot. Can you imagine someone so screwed up she'd spend seventeen hours making you a stupid poster and then turn around and get you fired? If you can figure that one out, you're better than me.

I spent the rest of the summer painting the neighbor's porches and keeping our pool clean. It was sort of a demotion, I guess, but at least I didn't have to work in depressing neighborhoods waiting on losers. I never saw Her Royal Lowness Charlene after that, but every once in a while I'd spot Doris at school. Usually it was in the cafeteria—there she'd be with about six or seven empty chairs around her. I'd be sitting with a bunch of guys laughing just loud enough so's she could hear what a good time sounded like. Once one of my friends caught her staring and began making these stupid pig snorts so that Doris looked away real quick. He kept it up, but instead of slugging him one, all's I did was stare down hard at the Formica tabletop like I was memorizing it. "Chill out," I finally said. "Just chill out."

I told my father the whole story right after I got canned, except leaving out the parts I thought would get me in trouble. We were out at the pool, him nursing his J&B and water and me floating belly-down on an air mattress. He listened to the whole thing and then hit me with this old clunker about how we often learn the most from painful situations. "Think of it as a learning experience, Eli. Do you know something that you hadn't known before?"

I tried hard to think of some smart-ass answer, the kind he can't stand, only nothing would come out. I just kept staring and staring down into that wobbly water.

# My *Tocaya*

SANDRA CISNEROS

Have you seen this girl? You must've seen her in the papers. Or then again at Father & Son's Taco Palace No. 2 on Nogalitos. Patricia Bernadette Benavídez, my *tocaya*, five feet, 115 pounds, thirteen years old.

Not that we were friends or anything like that. Sure we talked. But that was before she died and came back from the dead. Maybe you read about it or saw her on TV. She was on all the news channels. They interviewed anyone who knew her. Even the p.e. teacher who *had* to say nice things—*She was full of energy, a good kid, sweet*. Sweet as could be, considering she was a freak. Now why didn't anyone ask me?

Patricia Benavídez. The "son" half of Father & Son's Taco Palace No. 2 even before the son quit. That's how this Trish inherited the paper hat and white apron after school and every weekend, bored, a little sad, behind the high counters where customers ate standing up like horses.

That wasn't enough to make me feel sorry for her, though, even if her father *was* mean. But who could blame him? A girl who wore rhinestone earrings and glitter high heels to school was destined for trouble that nobody—not God or correctional institutions—could mend.

I think she got double promoted somewhere and that's how come she wound up in high school before she had any business being here. Yeah, kids like that always try too hard to fit in. Take this *tocaya*—same name as me, right? But does she call herself *la* Patee, or Patty, or something normal? No, she's gotta be different. Say's her name's "Trish." Invented herself a phony English accent too, all breathless and sexy like a British Marilyn Monroe. Real goofy. I mean, whoever heard of a Mexican with a British accent? Know what I mean? The girl had problems.

But if you caught her alone, and said, *Pa-trrri-see-ah—* I always made sure I said it in Spanish—*Pa-trrri-see-ah, cut the bull crap and be for real.* If you caught her without an audience, I guess she was all right.

That's how I managed to put up with her when I knew her, just before she ran away. Disappeared from a life sentence at that taco house. Got tired of coming home stinking of crispy tacos. Well, no wonder she left. I wouldn't want to stink of crispy tacos neither.

Who knows what she had to put up with. Maybe her father beat her. He beat the brother, I know that. Or at least they beat each other. It was one of those fistfights that finally did it—drove the boy off forever, though probably he was sick of stinking of tacos, too. That's what I'm thinking.

Then a few weeks after the brother was gone, this *tocaya* of mine had her picture in all the papers, just like the kids on milk cartons:

HAVE YOU SEEN THIS GIRL?
Patricia Bernadette Benavídez, 13, has been missing since Tuesday, Nov. 11, and her family is extremely worried. The girl, who is a student at Our Lady of Sorrows High School, is believed to be a runaway and was last seen on her way to school in the vicinity of Dolorosa and Soledad. Patricia is 5', 115 lbs., and was wearing a jean

jacket, blue plaid uniform skirt, white blouse, and high heels [*glitter probably*] when she disappeared. Her mother, Delfina Benavídez, has this message: "Honey, call Mommy y te quiero mucho."

Some people.

What did I care Benavídez disappeared? Wouldn't've. If it wasn't for Max Lucas Luna Luna, senior, Holy Cross, our brother school. They sometimes did exchanges with us. Teasers is what they were. Sex Rap Crap is what we called it, only the sisters called them different—Youth Exchanges. Like where they'd invite some of the guys from Holy Cross over here for Theology, and some of us girls from Sorrows would go over there. And we'd pretend like we were real interested in the issue "The Blessed Virgin: Role Model for Today's Young Woman," "Petting: Too Far, Too Fast, Too Late," "Heavy Metal and the Devil." Shit like that.

Not every day. Just once in a while as kind of an experiment. Catholic school was afraid of putting us all together too much, on account of hormones. That's what Sister Virginella said. If you can't conduct yourselves like proper young ladies when our guests arrive, we'll have to suspend our Youth Exchanges indefinitely. No whistling, grabbing, or stomping in the future, *is that clear?!!!*

Alls I know is he's got these little hips like the same size since he was twelve probably. Little waist and little ass wrapped up neat and sweet like a Hershey bar. Damn! That's what I remember.

Turns out Max Lucas Luna Luna lives next door to the freak. I mean, I never even bothered talking to Patricia Benavídez before, even though we were in the same section of General Business. But she comes up to me one day in the cafeteria when I'm waiting for my french fries and goes:

"Hey, *tocaya*, I know someone who's got the hots for you."

"Yeah, right," I says, trying to blow her off. I don't want to be seen talking to no flake.

"You know a guy named Luna from Holy Cross, the one who came over for that Theology exchange, the cute one with the ponytail?"

"So's?"

"Well, he and my brother Ralphie are tight, and he told Ralphie not to tell nobody but he thinks Patricia Chavez is real fine."

"You lie, girl."

"Swear to God. If you don't believe me, call my brother Ralphie."

That was enough to make me Trish Benavídez's best girlfriend for life, I swear. After that, I *always* made sure I got to General Business class early. Usually she'd have something to tell me, and if she didn't, I made sure to give her something to pass on to Max Lucas Luna Luna. But it was painful slow on account of this girl worked so much and didn't have no social life to speak of.

That's how this Patricia Bernadette got to be our messenger of luv-uv for a while, even though me and Max Lucas Luna Luna hadn't gotten beyond the I-like-you/Do-you-like-me stage. Hadn't so much as seen each other since the rap crap, but I was working on it.

I knew they lived somewhere in the Monte Vista area. So I'd ride my bike up and down streets—Magnolia, Mulberry, Huisache, Mistletoe—wondering if I was hot or cold. Just knowing Max Lucas Luna Luna might appear was enough to make my blood laugh.

The week I start dropping in at Father & Son's Taco Palace No. 2 is when she decides to skip. First we get an announcement over the intercom from Sister Virginella. *I am sorry to have to announce one of our youngest and dearest students has strayed from home. Let us keep her in our hearts and in our prayers until her safe return.* That's when she first got her picture in the paper with her ma's weepy message.

Personally it was no grief or relief to me she escaped so clean. That's for sure. But as it happened, she owed me. Bad enough she skips and has the whole school talking. At least *then* I had hope she'd make good on her promise to hook me up with Max Lucas Luna Luna. But just when I could say her name again without spitting, she goes and dies. Some kids playing in a drain ditch find a body, and yeah, it's her. When the TV cameras arrive at our school, there go all them drama hot shits howling real tears, even the ones that didn't know her. Sick.

Well, I couldn't help but feel bad for the dip once she's dead, right? I mean, after I got over being mad. Until she rose from the dead three days later.

After they've featured her ma crying into a wrinkled handkerchief and her dad saying, "She was my little princess," and the student body using money from our Padre Island field-trip fund to buy a bouquet of white glad-iolus with a banner that reads VIRGENCITA, CÚIDALA, and the whole damn school having to go to a high mass in her honor, my *tocaya* outdoes herself. Shows up at the down-town police station and says, I ain't dead.

Can you believe it? Her parents had identified the body in the morgue and everything. "I guess we were too upset to examine the body properly." Ha!

I never did get to meet Max Lucas Luna Luna, and who cares, right? All I'm saying is she couldn't even die right. But whose famous face is on the front page of the *San Antonio Light,* the *San Antonio Express News, and* the *Southside Reporter*? Girl, I'm telling you.

# Surrounded by Sleep

AKHIL SHARMA

One August afternoon, when Ajay was ten years old, his elder brother, Aman, dove into a pool and struck his head on the cement bottom. For three minutes, he lay there unconscious. Two boys continued to swim, kicking and splashing, until finally Aman was spotted below them. Water had entered through his nose and mouth. It had filled his stomach. His lungs collapsed. By the time he was pulled out, he could no longer think, talk, chew, or roll over in his sleep.

Ajay's family had moved from India to Queens, New York, two years earlier. The accident occurred during the boys' summer vacation, on a visit with their aunt and uncle in Arlington, Virginia. After the accident, Ajay's mother came to Arlington, where she waited to see if Aman would recover. At the hospital, she told the doctors and nurses that her son had been accepted into the Bronx High School of Science, in the hope that by highlighting his intelligence she would move them to make a greater effort on his behalf. Within a few weeks of the accident, the insurance company said that Aman should be transferred to a less expensive care facility, a long-term one. But only a few of these were any good, and those were full, and Ajay's mother refused to move Aman until a space opened in one of them. So she remained in Arlington, and Ajay stayed too, and his father visited from Queens on the weekends when he wasn't working. Ajay was enrolled at the local public school and in September he started fifth grade.

Before the accident, Ajay had never prayed much. In India, he and his brother used to go with their mother to the temple every Tuesday night, but that was mostly because there was a good *dosa* restaurant nearby. In America, his family went to a temple only on important holy days and birthdays. But shortly after Ajay's mother came to Arlington, she moved into the room that he and his brother had shared during the summer and made an altar in a corner. She threw an old flowered sheet over a cardboard box that had once held a television. On top she put a clay lamp, an incense-stick holder, and postcards depicting various gods. There was also a postcard of Mahatma Gandhi. She explained to Ajay that God could take any form; the picture of Mahatma Gandhi was there because he had appeared to her in a dream after the accident and told her that Aman would recover and become a surgeon. Now she and Ajay prayed for at least half an hour before the altar every morning and night.

At first she prayed with absolute humility. "Whatever you do will be good because you are doing it," she murmured to the postcards of Ram and Shivaji, daubing their lips with water and rice. Mahatma Gandhi got only water, because he did not like to eat. As weeks passed and Aman did not recover in time to return to the Bronx High School of Science for the first day of classes, his mother began doing things that called attention to her piety. She sometimes held the prayer lamp until it blistered her palms. Instead of kneeling before the altar, she lay face down. She fasted twice a week. Her attempts to sway God were not so different from Ajay's performing somersaults to amuse his aunt, and they made God seem human to Ajay.

One morning as Ajay knelt before the altar, he traced an Om, a crucifix, and a Star of David into the pile of the carpet. Beneath these he traced an S, for Superman, inside an upside-down triangle. His mother came up beside him.

"What are you praying for?" she asked. She had her hat on, a thick gray knitted one that a man might wear. The tracings went against the weave of the carpet and were darker than the surrounding nap. Pretending to examine them, Ajay leaned forward and put his hand over the S. His mother did not mind the Christian and Jewish symbols— they were for commonly recognized gods, after all—but she could not tolerate his praying to Superman. She'd caught him doing so once several weeks earlier and had become very angry, as if Ajay's faith in Superman made her faith in Ram ridiculous. "Right in front of God," she had said several times.

Ajay, in his nervousness, spoke the truth. "I'm asking God to give me a hundred percent on the math test."

His mother was silent for a moment. "What if God says you can have the math grade but then Aman will have to be sick a little while longer?" she asked.

Ajay kept quiet. He could hear cars on the road outside. He knew that his mother wanted to bewail her misfortune before God so that God would feel guilty. He looked at the postcard of Mahatma Gandhi. It was a black-and-white photo of him walking down a city street with an enormous crowd trailing behind him. Ajay thought of how, before the accident, Aman had been so modest that he would not leave the bathroom until he was fully dressed. Now he had rashes on his penis from the catheter that drew his urine into a translucent bag hanging from the guardrail of his bed.

His mother asked again, "Would you say, 'Let him be sick a little while longer'?"

"Are you going to tell me the story about Uncle Naveen again?" he asked.

"Why shouldn't I? When I was sick, as a girl, your uncle

walked seven times around the temple and asked God to let him fail his exams just as long as I got better."

"If I failed the math test and told you that story, you'd slap me and ask what one has to do with the other."

His mother turned to the altar. "What sort of sons did you give me, God?" she asked. "One you drown, the other is this selfish fool."

"I will fast today so that God puts some sense in me," Ajay said, glancing away from the altar and up at his mother. He liked the drama of fasting.

"No, you are a growing boy." His mother knelt down beside him and said to the altar, "He is stupid, but he has a good heart."

Prayer, Ajay thought, should appeal with humility and an open heart to some greater force. But the praying that he and his mother did felt sly and confused. By treating God as someone to bargain with, it seemed to him, they prayed as if they were casting a spell.

This meant that it was possible to do away with the presence of God entirely. For example, Ajay's mother had recently asked a relative in India to drive a nail into a holy tree and tie a saffron thread to the nail on Aman's behalf. Ajay invented his own ritual. On his way to school each morning, he passed a thick tree rooted half on the sidewalk and half on the road. One day Ajay got the idea that if he circled the tree seven times, touching the north side every other time, he would have a lucky day. From then on he did it every morning, although he felt embarrassed and always looked around beforehand to make sure no one was watching.

One night Ajay asked God whether he minded being prayed to only in need.

"You think of your toe only when you stub it," God replied. God looked like Clark Kent. He wore a gray cardigan, slacks, and thick glasses, and had a forelock that curled just as Ajay's did.

God and Ajay had begun talking occasionally after Aman drowned. Now they talked most nights while Ajay lay in bed and waited for sleep. God sat at the foot of Ajay's mattress. His mother's mattress lay parallel to his, a few feet away. Originally God had appeared to Ajay as Krishna, but Ajay had felt foolish discussing brain damage with a blue god who held a flute and wore a dhoti.

"You're not angry with me for touching the tree and all that?"

"No. I'm flexible."

"I respect you. The tree is just a way of praying to you," Ajay assured God.

God laughed. "I am not too caught up in formalities."

Ajay was quiet. He was convinced that he had been marked as special by Aman's accident. The beginnings of all heroes are distinguished by misfortune. Superman and Batman were both orphans. Krishna was separated from his parents at birth. The god Ram had to spend fourteen years in a forest. Ajay waited to speak until it would not appear improper to begin talking about himself.

"How famous will I be?" he asked finally.

"I can't tell you the future," God answered.

Ajay asked, "Why not?"

"Even if I told you something, later I might change my mind."

"But it might be harder to change your mind after you have said something will happen."

God laughed again. "You'll be so famous that fame will be a problem."

Ajay sighed. His mother snorted and rolled over.

"I want Aman's drowning to lead to something," he said to God.

"He won't be forgotten."

"I can't just be famous, though, I need to be rich too, to take care of Mummy and Daddy and pay Aman's hospital bills."

"You are always practical." God had a soulful and pitying voice, and God's sympathy made Ajay imagine himself as a truly tragic figure, like Amitabh Bachchan in the movie *Trishul*.

"I have responsibilities," Ajay said. He was so excited at the thought of his possible greatness that he knew he would have difficulty sleeping. Perhaps he would have to go read in the bathroom.

"You can hardly imagine the life ahead," God said.

Even though God's tone promised greatness, the idea of the future frightened Ajay. He opened his eyes. There was a light coming from the street. The room was cold and had a smell of must and incense. His aunt and uncle's house was a narrow two-story home next to a four-lane road. The apartment building with the pool where Aman had drowned was a few blocks up the road, one in a cluster of tall brick buildings with stucco fronts. Ajay pulled the blanket tighter around him. In India, he could not have imagined the reality of his life in America: the thick smell of meat in the school cafeteria, the many television channels. And, of course, he could not have imagined Aman's accident, or the hospital where he spent so much time.

The hospital was boring. Vinod, Ajay's cousin, picked him up after school and dropped him off there almost every day. Vinod was twenty-two. In addition to attending county college and studying computer programming, he worked at a 7-Eleven near Ajay's school. He often brought Ajay hot chocolate and a comic from the store, which had to be returned, so Ajay was not allowed to open it until he had wiped his hands.

Vinod usually asked him a riddle on the way to the hospital. "Why are manhole covers round?" It took Ajay half the ride to admit that he did not know. He was having difficulty talking. He didn't know why. The only time he could talk easily was when he was with God. The explanation he gave himself for this was that just as he couldn't chew when there was too much in his mouth, he couldn't talk when there were too many thoughts in his head.

When Ajay got to Aman's room, he greeted him as if he were all right. "Hello, lazy. How much longer are you going to sleep?" His mother was always there. She got up and hugged Ajay. She asked how school had been, and he didn't know what to say. In music class, the teacher sang a song about a sailor who had bared his breast before jumping into the sea. This had caused the other students to giggle. But Ajay could not say the word *breast* to his mother without blushing. He had also cried. He'd been thinking of how Aman's accident had made his own life mysterious and confused. What would happen next? Would Aman die or would he go on as he was? Where would they live? Usually when Ajay cried in school, he was told to go outside. But it had been raining, and the teacher had sent him into the hallway. He sat on the floor and wept. Any mention of this would upset his mother. And so he said nothing had happened that day.

Sometimes when Ajay arrived his mother was on the phone, telling his father that she missed him and was expecting to see him on Friday. His father took a Greyhound bus most Fridays from Queens to Arlington, returning on Sunday night in time to work the next day. He was a bookkeeper for a department store. Before the accident, Ajay had thought of his parents as the same person: MummyDaddy. Now, when he saw his father praying stiffly or when his father failed to say hello to Aman in his hospital bed, Ajay sensed that his mother and father were quite different people. After his mother got off the phone, she always went to the cafeteria to get coffee for herself and Jell-O or cookies for him. He knew that if she took her coat with her, it meant she was especially sad. Instead of going directly to the cafeteria, she was going to go outside and walk around the hospital parking lot.

That day, while she was gone, Ajay stood beside the hospital bed and balanced a comic book on Aman's chest. He read to him very slowly. Before turning each page, he said, "Okay, Aman?"

Aman was fourteen. He was thin and had curly hair. Immediately after the accident, there had been so many machines around his bed that only one person could stand beside him at a time. Now there was just a single waxy yellow tube. One end of this went into his abdomen; the other, blocked by a green bullet-shaped plug, was what his Isocal milk was poured through. When not being used, the tube was rolled up and bound by a rubber band and tucked beneath Aman's hospital gown. But even with the tube hidden, it was obvious that there was something wrong with Aman. It was in his stillness and his open eyes. Once, in their home in Queens, Ajay had left a plastic bowl on a radiator overnight and the sides had drooped and sagged so that the bowl looked a little like an eye. Aman reminded Ajay of that bowl.

Ajay had not gone with his brother to the swimming pool on the day of the accident, because he had been reading a book and wanted to finish it. But he heard the ambulance siren from his aunt and uncle's house. The pool was only a few minutes away, and when he got there a crowd had gathered around the ambulance. Ajay saw his uncle first, in shorts and an undershirt, talking to a man inside the ambulance. His aunt was standing beside him. Then Ajay saw Aman on a stretcher, in blue shorts with a plastic mask over his nose and mouth. His aunt hurried over to take Ajay home. He cried as they walked, although he had been certain that Aman would be fine in a few days: in a Spider-Man comic he had just read, Aunt May had fallen into a coma and she had woken up perfectly fine. Ajay had cried simply because he felt crying was called for by the seriousness of the occasion. Perhaps this moment would mark the beginning of his future greatness. From that day on, Ajay found it hard to cry in front of his family. Whenever tears started coming, he felt like a liar. If he loved his brother, he knew, he would not have thought about himself as the ambulance had pulled away, nor would he talk with God at night about becoming famous.

When Ajay's mother returned to Aman's room with coffee and cookies, she sometimes talked to Ajay about Aman. She told him that when Aman was six he had seen a children's television show that had a character named Chunu, which was Aman's nickname, and he had thought the show was based on his own life. But most days Ajay went into the lounge to read. There was a TV in the corner and a lamp near a window that looked out over a parking lot. It was the perfect place to read. Ajay liked fantasy novels where the hero, who was preferably under the age of twenty-five, had an undiscovered talent that made him famous when it was revealed. He could read for hours without interruption, and sometimes when Vinod came to drive Ajay and his mother home from the hospital it was hard for him to remember the details of the real day that had passed.

One evening when he was in the lounge, he saw a rock star being interviewed on *Entertainment Tonight*. The musician, dressed in a sleeveless undershirt that revealed a swarm of tattoos on his arms and shoulders, had begun to shout at the audience, over his interviewer, "Don't watch me! Live your life! I'm not you!" Filled with a sudden desire to do something, Ajay hurried out of the television lounge and stood on the sidewalk in front of the hospital entrance. But he did not know what to do. It was cold and dark and there was an enormous moon. Cars leaving the parking lot stopped one by one at the edge of the road. Ajay watched as they waited for an opening in the traffic, their brake lights glowing.

"Are things getting worse?" Ajay asked God. The weekend before had been Thanksgiving. Christmas soon would come, and a new year would start, a year during which Aman would not have talked or walked. Suddenly Ajay understood hopelessness. Hopelessness felt very much like fear. It involved a clutching in the stomach and a numbness in the arms and legs.

"What do you think?" God answered.

"They seem to be."

"At least Aman's hospital hasn't forced him out."

"At least Aman isn't dead. At least Daddy's Greyhound bus has never skidded off a bridge." Lately Ajay had begun talking much more quickly to God than he used to. Before, when he had talked to God, Ajay would think of what God would say in response before he said anything. Now Ajay spoke without knowing how God might respond.

"You shouldn't be angry at me." God sighed. God was wearing his usual cardigan. "You can't understand why I do what I do."

"You should explain better, then."

"Christ was my son. I loved Job. How long did Ram have to live in a forest?"

"What does that have to do with me?" This was usually the cue for discussing Ajay's prospects. But hopelessness made the future feel even more frightening than the present.

"I can't tell you what the connection is, but you'll be proud of yourself."

They were silent for a while.

"Do you love me truly?" Ajay asked.

"Yes."

"Will you make Aman normal?" As soon as Ajay asked the question, God ceased to be real. Ajay knew then that he was alone, lying under his blankets, his faced exposed to the cold dark.

"I can't tell you the future," God said softly. These were words that Ajay already knew.

"Just get rid of the minutes when Aman lay on the bottom of the pool. What are three minutes to you?"

"Presidents die in less time than that. Planes crash in less time than that."

Ajay opened his eyes. His mother was on her side and she had a blanket pulled up to her neck. She looked like an ordinary woman. It surprised him that you couldn't tell, looking at her, that she had a son who was brain-dead.

In fact, things were getting worse. Putting away his mother's mattress and his own in a closet in the morning, getting up very early so he could use the bathroom before his aunt or uncle did, spending so many hours at the hospital—all this had given Ajay the reassuring sense that real life was in abeyance, and that what was happening was unreal. He and his mother and brother were just waiting to make a long-delayed bus trip. The bus would come eventually to carry them to Queens, where he would return to school at P.S. 20 and to Sunday afternoons spent at the Hindi movie theater under the trestle for the 7 train. But now Ajay was starting to understand that the world was always real, whether you were reading a book or sleeping, and that it eroded you every day.

He saw the evidence of this erosion in his mother, who had grown severe and unforgiving. Usually when Vinod brought her and Ajay home from the hospital, she had dinner with the rest of the family. After his mother helped his aunt wash the dishes, the two women watched theological action movies. One night, in spite of a headache that had made her sit with her eyes closed all afternoon, she ate dinner, washed dishes, sat down in front of the TV. As soon as the movie was over, she went upstairs, vomited, and lay on her mattress with a wet towel over her fore-head. She asked Ajay to massage her neck and shoulders. As he did so, Ajay noticed that she was crying. The tears frightened Ajay and made him angry. "You shouldn't have watched TV," he said accusingly.

"I have to," she said. "People will cry with you once, and they will cry with you a second time. But if you cry a third time, people will say you are boring and always crying."

Ajay did not want to believe what she had said, but her cynicism made him think that she must have had conver-sations with his aunt and uncle that he did not know about. "That's not true," he told her, massaging her scalp. "Uncle is kind, Auntie Aruna is always kind."

"What do you know?" She shook her head, freeing her-self from Ajay's fingers. She stared at him. Upside down, her face looked unfamiliar and terrifying. "If God lets Aman live long enough, you will become a stranger too. You will say, 'I have been unhappy for so long because of Aman, now I don't want to talk about him or look at him.' Don't think I don't know you," she said.

Suddenly Ajay hated himself. To hate himself was to see himself as the opposite of everything he wanted to be: short instead of tall, fat instead instead of thin. When he brushed his teeth that night, he looked at his face: his chin was round and fat as a heel. His nose was so broad that he had once been able to fit a small rock in one nostril.

His father was also being eroded. Before the accident, Ajay's father loved jokes—he could do perfect imita-tions—and Ajay had felt lucky to have him as a father. (Once, Ajay's father had convinced his own mother that he was possessed by the ghost of a British man.) And even after the accident, his father had impressed Ajay with the patient loyalty of his weekly bus journeys. But now his father was different.

One Saturday afternoon, as Ajay and his father were returning from the hospital, his father slowed the car without warning and turned into the dirt parking lot of a bar that looked as though it had originally been a small house. It had a pitched roof with a black tarp. At the edge of the lot stood a tall neon sign of an orange hand lifting a mug of sudsy golden beer. Ajay had never seen anybody drink except in the movies. He wondered whether his father was going to ask for directions to somewhere, and if so, to where.

His father said, "One minute," and they climbed out of the car.

They went up wooden steps into the bar. Inside, it was dark and smelled of cigarette smoke and something stale and sweet. The floor was linoleum like the kitchen at his aunt and uncle's. There was a bar with stools around it, and a basketball game played on a television bolted against the ceiling, like the one in Aman's hospital room.

His father stood by the bar waiting for the bartender to notice him. His father had a round face and was wearing a white shirt and dark dress pants, as he often did on the weekend, since it was more economical to have the same clothes for the office and home.

The bartender came over. "How much for a Budweiser?" his father asked.

It was a dollar fifty. "Can I buy a single cigarette?" He did not have to buy; the bartender would just give him one. His father helped Ajay up onto a stool and sat down himself. Ajay looked around and wondered what would happen if somebody started a knife fight. When his father had drunk half his beer, he carefully lit the cigarette. The bartender was standing at the end of the bar. There were only two other men in the place. Ajay was disappointed that there were no women wearing dresses slit all the way up their thighs. Perhaps they came in the evenings.

His father asked him if he had ever watched a basketball game all the way through.

"I've seen the Harlem Globetrotters."

His father smiled and took a sip. "I've heard they don't play other teams, because they can defeat everyone else so easily."

"They only play against each other, unless there is an emergency—like in the cartoon, when they play against the aliens to save the Earth," Ajay said.

"Aliens?"

Ajay blushed as he realized his father was teasing him.

When they left, the light outside felt too bright. As his father opened the car door for Ajay, he said. "I'm sorry." That's when Ajay first felt that his father might have done something wrong. The thought made him worry. Once they were on the road, his father said gently, "Don't tell your mother."

Fear made Ajay feel cruel. He asked his father, "What do you think about when you think of Aman?"

Instead of becoming sad, Ajay's father smiled. "I am surprised by how strong he is. It's not easy for him to keep living. But even before, he was strong. When he was interviewing for high school scholarships, one interviewer asked him, 'Are you a thinker or a doer?' He laughed and said, 'That's like asking, 'Are you an idiot or a moron?'"

From then on they often stopped at the bar on the way back from the hospital. Ajay's father always asked the bartender for a cigarette before he sat down, and during the ride home he always reminded Ajay not to tell his mother.

Ajay found that he himself was changing. His superstitions were becoming extreme. Now when he walked around the good-luck tree he punched it, every other time, hard, so that his knuckles hurt. Afterward, he would hold his breath for a moment longer than he thought he could bear, and ask God to give the unused breaths to Aman.

In December, a place opened in one of the good long-term care facilities. It was in New Jersey. This meant that Ajay and his mother could move back to New York and live with his father again. This was the news Ajay's father brought when he arrived for a two-week holiday at Christmas.

Ajay felt the clarity of panic. Life would be the same as before the accident but also unimaginably different. He would return to P.S. 20, while Aman continued to be fed through a tube in his abdomen. Life would be Aman's getting older and growing taller than their parents but having less consciousness than even a dog, which can become excited or afraid.

Ajay decided to use his devotion to shame God into fixing Aman. The fact that two religions regarded the coming December days as holy ones suggested to Ajay that prayers during this time would be especially potent. So he prayed whenever he thought of it—at his locker, even in the middle of a quiz. His mother wouldn't let him fast, but he started throwing away the lunch he took to school. And when his mother prayed in the morning, Ajay watched to make sure that she bowed at least once toward each of the postcards of deities. If she did not, he bowed three times to the possibly offended god on the postcard. He had noticed that his father finished his prayers in less time than it took to brush his teeth. And so now, when his father began praying in the morning, Ajay immediately crouched down beside him, because he knew his father would be embarrassed to get up first. But Ajay found it harder and harder to drift into the rhythm of sung prayers or into his nightly conversations with God. How could chanting and burning incense undo three minutes of a sunny August afternoon? It was like trying to move a sheet of blank paper from one end of a table to the other by blinking so fast that you started a breeze.

On Christmas Eve his mother asked the hospital chaplain to come to Aman's room and pray with them. The family knelt together beside Aman's bed. Afterward the chaplain asked her whether she would be attending Christmas services. "Of course, Father," she said.

"I'm also coming," Ajay said.

The chaplain turned toward Ajay's father, who was sitting in a wheelchair because there was nowhere else to sit.

"I'll wait for God at home," he said.

That night, Ajay watched *It's a Wonderful Life* on television. To him, the movie meant that happiness arrived late, if ever. Later, when he got in bed and closed his eyes, God appeared. There was little to say.

"Will Aman be better in the morning?"

"No."

"Why not?"

"When you prayed for the math exam, you could have asked for Aman to get better, and instead of your getting an A, Aman would have woken."

This was so ridiculous that Ajay opened his eyes. His father was sleeping nearby on folded-up blankets. Ajay felt disappointed at not feeling guilt. Guilt might have contained some hope that God existed.

When Ajay arrived at the hospital with his father and mother the next morning, Aman was asleep, breathing through his mouth while a nurse poured a can of Isocal into his stomach through the yellow tube. Ajay had not expected that Aman would have recovered; nevertheless, seeing him that way put a weight in Ajay's chest.

The Christmas prayers were held in a large, mostly empty room: people in chairs sat next to people in wheelchairs. His father walked out in the middle of the service.

Later, Ajay sat in a corner of Aman's room and watched his parents. His mother was reading a Hindi women's magazine to Aman while she shelled peanuts in her lap. His father was reading a thick red book in preparation for a civil service exam. The day wore on. The sky outside grew dark. At some point Ajay began to cry. He tried to be quiet. He did not want his parents to notice his tears and think that he was crying for Aman, because in reality he was crying for how difficult his own life was.

His father noticed first. "What's the matter, hero?"

His mother shouted, "What happened?" and she sounded so alarmed it was as if Ajay were bleeding.

"I didn't get any Christmas presents. I need a Christmas present," Ajay shouted. "You didn't buy me a Christmas present." And then, because he had revealed his own selfishness, Ajay let himself sob. "You have to give me something. I should get something for all this." Ajay clenched his hands and wiped his face with his fists. "Each time I come here I should get something."

His mother pulled him up and pressed him into her stomach. His father came and stood beside them. "What do you want?" his father asked.

Ajay had no prepared answer for this.

"What do you want?" his mother repeated.

The only thing he could think was "I want to eat pizza and I want candy."

His mother stroked his hair and called him her little baby. She kept wiping his face with a fold of her sari. When at last he stopped crying, they decided that Ajay's father should take him back to his aunt and uncle's. On the way, they stopped at a mini-mall. It was a little after five, and the streetlights were on. Ajay and his father did not take off their winter coats as they ate, in a pizzeria staffed by Chinese people. While he chewed, Ajay closed his eyes and tried to imagine God looking like Clark Kent, wearing a cardigan and eyeglasses, but he could not. Afterward, Ajay and his father went next door to a magazine shop and Ajay got a bag of Three Musketeers bars and a bag of Reese's peanut butter cups, and then he was tired and ready for home.

He held the candy in his lap while his father drove in silence. Even through the plastic, he could smell the sugar and chocolate. Some of the houses outside were dark, and others were outlined in Christmas lights.

After a while Ajay rolled down the window slightly. The car filled with wind. They passed the building where Aman's accident had occurred. Ajay had not walked past it since the accident. When they drove by, he usually looked away. Now he tried to spot the fenced swimming pool at the building's side. He wondered whether the pool that had pressed itself into Aman's mouth and lungs and stomach had been drained, so that nobody would be touched by its unlucky waters. Probably it had not been emptied until fall. All summer long, people must have swum in the pool and sat on its sides, splashing their feet in the water, and not known that his brother had lain for three minutes on its concrete bottom one August afternoon.

# One Extra Parking Space

JACQUELINE SHEEHAN

Thomas is my twin brother. Everyone asks, "Are you fraternal or identical twins?" Jesus, just one look at us and how could anyone ask if we are identical? I am a girl with blonde hair. Thomas is a boy with dark brown hair. I have brown eyes; he has blue eyes. My skin is the good kind that tans. His skin has freckles and burns so easy that I've seen his back pickle up with blisters. Also, I'm in all the smart classes, and he's retarded.

We came from the same womb at the same time. Everything went right in my side of the cooker, especially when our brains were getting hard-wired, and everything possible went wrong with Thomas's brain.

He has one extra chromosome. Whenever I see pictures of chromosomes, they look like pairs of parking spaces stacked on top of one another. Thomas got one extra parking space thrown in, and the result is some very screwy wiring in his brain.

I used to think, when I was little, that Thomas was just kidding, and that one day he was going to let us know how smart he really was. I used to dream that he and I could drive racecars and we would win the grand prize. We would both drive wild and fast.

Thomas has Down's Syndrome. He will never in his lifetime be able to make change. If he goes into a store, he pays for everything with a twenty-dollar bill, because so far nothing has ever cost more than twenty dollars and so he always gets money back, which he likes. He buys a lot of batteries. The best batteries are nine volts, the kind that come in a rectangular shape. His battery collection is kind of weird, but then, so is Thomas. Batteries are like the best baseball cards in the world to him. He buys other batteries, like the kind you put in flashlights.

Dad says, "I sure could use some new batteries for my flashlight. I wonder where I could get some?" Thomas raises his hand and shouts, "I have batteries!" He has a thick, lispy way of speaking because his tongue is too much for his mouth. Thomas runs to his room and sorts through his display shelf of batteries and gets Dad the right kind. He is reluctant to give out his prized nine-volt batteries.

There is nobody who knows Thomas better than I do. When we took naps together before I went to kindergarten, I would stay awake until I heard his snuffling breathing even out. Then I would lay my face next to his so that when it was time to wake up, the first thing we would see was each other.

In a couple of years, I'll go to college. I have been telling him about college. He has a problem understanding time. It's like he lives in another universe where all things are now. When I first told him about college, he cried all night because he thought I was leaving the next day.

"No, Thomas. Not until I'm eighteen. Right now I'm only sixteen. That are two more years," I said, holding up two fingers.

He put his hands on his hips and said, "I'm not stupid. I know how fast two is. Two is like this," and he clapped his hands together. Handclapping is Thomas's concession to his inability to snap his fingers.

Now that I can drive, I take him shopping with me, which gives Mom a break because he can be hard to shop with. Mom used to come home from shopping for school clothes with Thomas and the crease between her eyebrows was deep and dark. For the last five years, he would wear only one kind of shirt, a short-sleeved shirt with two pockets and the Penney's logo had to be embroidered on one pocket. Of course, I know exactly what he likes.

Nobody but me knows Thomas in the true, spit-tasting kind of way. On the way home from Penney's, when I was driving wild down I-84, he said, "Two goes fast, Lizbeth."

"Two what?"

"Two years!"

Two years is forever to me. It's my junior and senior years of high school and everyone knows how wicked long that is, especially if you have Pre-calculus and Trig and Latin IV. So I showed Thomas on the dashboard of our Toyota.

"Look, this whole dashboard is two years. Here's *now* on the left side and this nickel is me. This penny way over on your side of the car is me going to college. Every day I will show you how the nickel moves, and Thomas, it will move very, very slowly."

You never know when an idea is going to grab him. Thomas went over the top with the dashboard idea. He took two of his double-A batteries and taped them together, with yellow yarn glued on the tip of one and brown yarn glued on the tip of the other. The yellow one is me, with Thomas on the left side. Mom helped him superglue a long strip of Velcro across the full length of the dashboard and she put the grabbing part of the Velcro on the bottom of the Thomas and Lizbeth twin battery ensemble.

Other points in time were important. Our birthdays were balloons painted on with purple nail polish. Christmases were two bristly trees from our old toy box in the attic. Halloweens were marked by acorns painted orange with black eyes.

The Toyota was eleven years old and my parents had

always said that it would be my car when I started to drive. I told Thomas it was our car. He washed it every other day. He also learned to check the oil. Sometimes he checked the oil three or four times a day. He would say, very loudly in case any of the neighbors were hard of hearing, "I'm going to check the oil on my car now."

By the end of the summer before my junior year, the Thomas/Lizbeth double-A battery dolls had moved to the right about one-and-a-half inches. He and I drove our Toyota to the Dairy Queen run by Jerry, the bald-headed guy. Jerry always remembered Thomas.

"How's my man Thomas?"

Thomas pushed his head into the air-conditioned Dairy Queen window.

"I have to check the oil on my car, Jerry."

Thomas popped the lid and fiddled elaborately with the dipstick while I ordered two hot-fudge sundaes. I was sliding my change into my pocket when I heard the trouble start.

"Hey, check my oil, too."

Two boys with backwards baseball caps elbowed each other in their Ford pickup. Thomas's eyes lit up.

"Sure," said Thomas.

"Oh shit, he's coming over here. Are you gonna let that retard touch your truck?"

My blood thumped faster through my head, and I whirled around. I was at their truck window before I knew that my legs had moved.

"Are you asking my brother to check your oil?"

"Your brother? I thought maybe he was your boyfriend."

It was such a stupid thing to say that I couldn't find a comeback. And Thomas was watching, smiling, thinking that they really wanted him to check under their big, fat hood. So I told Thomas not to check his oil, that we were leaving.

Thomas ate his hot-fudge sundae as we drove. Mine sat

in a white paper bag. I was picturing a set of slashed tires on a Ford pickup, hot fudge in the air-filter, me wrestling those boys to the ground, telling them to never, never make fun of my brother again.

"You're mad, Lizbeth, I can tell."

"I'm not mad at you."

He was quiet for a few moments, carving craters into his ice cream. I was thinking about how I was going to protect him when I went away to college.

"Lizbeth, when you go to college, you will have to check your own oil. I can't always be there to do it for you."

He was looking at me with his head tilted to the side. He had hot fudge on his lips.

"And you will have to let me check the oil on other cars. Two years will come and you will have to be ready," he said.

# Laughing in the Dark

RAND RICHARDS COOPER

All last spring I was depressed. Even when I felt OK, the OK-ness was like a paper-thin membrane, and feeling bad was beating hard underneath. I knew something was wrong with me. Sometime during the winter, just when everyone else had shifted up a gear, I'd gone into neutral. At school I'd get a pass to the library and sit in a carrel with the college application essays I was supposed to be doing. *Describe two people who have influenced you. Tell about an event that had an important effect on you.* I'd just sit there, staring. And it wasn't only this. It was other things, like how when Mr. Latimer was telling me *I'm not going to let you fall through the cracks, Danny*, he glanced toward the Faculty Room and I knew he was picturing his next cigarette.

It was a lot of stupid little nothings that somehow added up to everything.

May 11th was part of it too—my sister Janice's birthday. Janice ran away from home after a fight with my father when she was fifteen and I was four, and I never saw her again. It's not a topic anyone talks about, but last spring I was obsessing about it. I'd come home and find my mother at her easel in the front room. It's something she started after she and my father got divorced. Her paintings are scenes of boats and beaches, mountains and waterfalls, with terrific details—butterflies in the background, or the petals of a daisy lying in a pile. She uses a magnifying glass. She sits close to the canvas, biting on the end of her paintbrush. When I hear her sigh, I know she's using the magnifying glass. Somehow that made me feel even worse. I'd go up to my room and stand in front of the mirror, pulling my eye-bags off my eye, like they do to Malcolm MacDowell in *A Clockwork Orange*, and watching my eye become completely round like a ping-pong ball.

But then I imagined Angela Tourtelotte's honking little voice going "Oh gross, that's like, so *twisted!*" So I stopped.

The thing with Ms. Angela T. had begun two months before, in March, when Mr. Latimer decided I needed an "assistant" for my senior project on Social Intelligence—a portfolio of photos showing people whose relationships other people in test groups had to guess at. Latimer gave my name to a kid who was writing a Most Compatible Person program for his project. I lied blatantly on the questionnaire. Yes, I loved junk food and football, and yes, men *should* open doors for women "out of respect." When the list came back, the girl for me was a tenth grader named Angela Tourtelotte.

I went down to introduce myself. Angela Tourtelotte must have done some serious lying on the questionnaire too, because she did not look like someone who wanted doors opened for her out of respect. She was into some Retro Punk act—hair shaved on one side, six earrings, plastic handcuff belt, and bowling shoes, the green and red ones with the big numbers on the back. I asked her: "You really think people trust someone in bowling shoes?"

She made a honking noise like post-nasal drip. Was that her laugh? I wanted to know.

"God, let's be boring!" She banged her locker shut and walked away.

For some reason we started hanging out anyway. First we went around taking photos for my project. Her strategy was to hover like a vulture, then swoop up to someone and say, "Hi, we'd like to take your picture!" When people asked what she wanted them to do, she said: "Just walk like you were walking. Just be you." They loved it. I circled around, snapping and clicking.

*You'll be a famous photographer and be on "Oprah,"* Angela T told me. *You'll go across America and do a book about people who look like their gerbils!*

I liked going over to her house. It was always loud, with the twins, Ricky and Mickey, cruising around yelling "Do the Giants rule, or *what?!*" and the dog, Ralph, barking, and the TV on, and Mrs. Tourtelotte shouting for a little HELP here, please! in the kitchen. Mr. T was always slapping me on the back. *This is the first normal person you've brought around here in years, Angie,* he said. *Stick around, lemme enjoy it a little!*

For someone supposedly so punk, Angela Tourtelotte had some pretty homey ideas. Like humming the theme song from *Leave It to Beaver* and calling people "Wally" and "Beave." Or riding go-carts at Kart-O-Rama, or keeping a lock of her mother's hair in a little silver box. I asked her, did Mommy serve her cookies and milk after school?

"Don't be a Wally," she said.

Sometimes Mrs. Tourtelotte let us use her car. Angela Tourtelotte's idea of a terrific Saturday night was to cruise past her friends' houses in the Estate Wagon, putting purple lipstick on in the visor mirror and blasting music on the tape deck—horrible bands like King Missile. She begged me to let her drive. She'd have her license in six months, so what was the big deal? I told her I didn't think she'd get her license.

"Oh yeah? Well I'll be sixteen, and that's the law, Wally."

"Not in your case. In your case they'll make an exception."

"Why in my case?"

"Because," I said, "you're dangerous. You're a public menace."

She liked that. She slid over and whispered, "I'm public enemy number one!" and kind of nuzzled into my shoulder.

"Hey," I said. "I'm driving." And she went back over to her side.

I was only seventeen, so there was no law against doing with Angela Tourtelotte all the things everyone always talks about doing. But I never knew whether they really did those things. When I thought about two people doing it, I always got this image of fish flopping on a dock—curling back and forth and sucking air and slowly dying. One Saturday after the driving incident, Angela Tourtelotte dragged me to Kart-O-Rama, where we raced around like maniacs with a bunch of ten-year-olds. In the middle of it, she pulled her cart over and waved me alongside, like she wanted to tell me something. Then, instead, she stuck her tongue in my ear.

I knew I was supposed to be experiencing maximum passion, but all I could think was, Who *is* this person with her tongue in my ear?

My father called and asked me to lunch. We met at the Fast Attack Deli, by the Boat Works. My father designs ventilator systems for submarines.

"So, Danny," he said when our grinders came. "Tell me what your plans are these days."

I babbled about the photos Angela T and I were taking for my project.

"That's a hobby," he broke in. "You can do that in your free time." In exactly three weeks, he reminded me, I was graduating. He was wondering what I was planning to do.

"Maybe I'll travel," I said. "Go across America and take pictures."

"Pictures?"

"You know. Photographs. I'll make a book out of it."

When he's stressed out, my father runs his hand over his bald head in an Ancient Hair Reflex. "Do I sense your mother behind this?" he asked.

I didn't need Mom to make my plans for me, I told him. "It's my life, you know."

"Yes, son. Yes, it is." He heaved a sigh that made it sound truly sad, even to me, that it *was* my life. Then he went on, talking about some medical-technician training program a friend of his had gotten his son into. I started thinking about Janice. When she ran away, my parents hired a detective. But after three years my father decided enough was enough. He told my mother to clear out Janice's room. She took down the horse drawings and Woodstock posters, rolled them up and tied them with red ribbons.

"You're not listening, Danny," my father said.

"Dad," I said. "Where do you think she is right now?" I wanted him to say her name, just once. I wanted to see his lips make the motion.

"I'm sitting here trying to help, and you're not even—"

I aimed it right at him, point-blank: "You can't even say her name, can you?"

"Son, I don't think—"

"You can't! She ran away because of you, and you can't even say her name! Janice! Janice!"

I was shouting, and people stared. My father turned away, then changed his mind and came back hard with a finger in my face. "Now you listen to me, son. Your sister made her decision. She abandoned her family and threw herself on the mercy of strangers."

I tried to break in, but he held up his hand. "It was a damned foolish thing to do, but if you want to worship it, that's your business. In the meantime, I suggest you do some hard thinking about your own situation."

He took a ten-dollar bill from his wallet and tossed it on the table, then walked away.

After he left, I sat for a long time looking out the window across Sub Way to the Boat Works. It's like a city over there. There are brick buildings and glass buildings and a massive green building where the subs are built. There's a huge sign shaped like a sub that says SUBMARINE CAPITAL OF THE WORLD in pink neon letters.

All spring I'd been wondering what was going through Janice's mind the day she ran away. She must have had a good reason for going, I believed. When I tried to imagine where she could be, I always pictured her in some green and breezy place, with horses. In my mind it was Montana, but not really Montana—not Montana itself. I saw her standing in the sunlight, swinging her leg up over a big, reddish-brown horse. She'd start to ride off, toward a mountain. I'd go closer and try to get a look at her face, but the sunlight coming over the mountain was too bright.

The bill was $9.15, so I added another dollar to my father's cheapskate ten, and the waitress took it away. I put on my jacket and left. Out on Sub Way I took a last look at the shipyard. I thought about the weeks and months and years and decades my father had spent going there.

Maybe he was right about Janice, I thought. But the funny thing was, he still hadn't said her name.

The night everything finally caved in, we were at Angela Tourtelotte's, babysitting. Her parents were out at a restaurant, and the twins were in bed. Around eleven we were watching *Magnificent Obsession,* the old version with Robert Taylor, where he becomes a brain surgeon just to save the life of this girl he loves. Angela Tourtelotte was sitting next to me on the couch.

"You know what?" she said. "You should do something wild and totally weird your father out."

"Like what? Become a brain surgeon and give him a brain transplant?"

"No!" She gave me her Sweeping Scorn look. "I mean something dangerous. Like, I don't know—going and becoming a male stripper and dancing in some bar for frustrated housewives, or something."

"Gee," I said. "Great idea!"

"God, I was just *kidding!*" She took the remote control and fast-forwarded, making everything ridiculous. I stared at her. "Hi there," she said, batting her eyelashes. Her face came toward mine. We kissed, sort of. She pulled back, licking her lips like she was trying to figure out what I tasted like.

"Do you always get so nervous?" she said.

"I'm not nervous."

"Yes you are." She looked at me. "Aha!" she said. "A virgin!" She burrowed her face into my neck, yelling *the Virgin Danny!* over and over.

"Hey, come on." I pushed her away. "Cut it out."

When Angela Tourtelotte gets mad, it happens fast, the switch just gets flipped. "You're always rejecting me, you know," she said. "Like, totally."

"No," I said. "Look, it's just . . ."

"You think I'm hideous or something, right? You think all this stuff is totally bogus!" She was pulling off her plastic bracelets. "It's not like I was born with all this crap on, you know!" She started in on her earrings, and I was afraid she was going to rip right through her ear.

"Look," I said. "I'm not rejecting you." I just didn't want to wake up the twins, I told her. And weren't we supposed to be watching a movie, anyway?

Angela sighed and rolled her eyes. "You're like an old man," she said. "Look at you. Don't you ever get happy?"

Sure I did, I said. Everyone got happy sometime, didn't they?

"No, not like *that*. I mean HAPPY! I mean screaming and yelling happy! Obnoxious happy! Freak-out-people-on-the-street happy!" She stared at me.

"Think about it," she said.

I did think about it. We sat there watching the movie, and I thought about it and thought about it.

At some point the door opened, and Angela's parents barged in.

"Hiya gang!" said Mr. T. "Everything OK here at the ranch?"

Instantly Angela Tourtelotte had her earrings and bracelets gathered up in an inconspicuous pile. "Yeah," she said. "But poophead here wouldn't let me drive the car, even though I *told* him you'd let me."

"My ass I would," Mr. T said.

"Jack!" Mrs. Tourtelotte pretended to be shocked.

"OK then," he said, "*your* ass I would!" He pinched her, and she slapped his hand away.

"I gotta go," I said, and stood up.

Mr. Tourtelotte took me home. He was one of those drivers who steer with their wrists resting on the crossbars of the steering wheel. Even at the sharp corners he never actually grabbed the wheel with his hand. He started telling me about his paving company, JT Pavers. The only reason he'd started the company, he said, was so that if Mrs. T. ever got involved in any hanky-panky with anyone, the guy would find himself "permanently parked" at Stop N Shop— beneath the parking lot. "You take a look at that lot sometime, Dan. Northwest corner, twenty-thirty feet in."

We drove along. Every time a band of light from the streetlights went by, I saw Mr. Tourtelotte smiling, as if he was remembering a great joke. "So," he said, "Angie behaving herself these days?" I didn't know what to say, and he kept talking. "Christ, she puts any more metal in that ear of hers, she's gonna start picking up radio signals!" He laughed softly.

The house was dark when we pulled in. "Thanks a lot for the ride," I said.

He leaned close, and I could smell whatever he'd been drinking, rum or something. "Dan," he said. "I'll let you in on a little secret." Suddenly I thought, maybe he really *did* bury some guy at the Stop N Shop.

"It's hard to be bad," he whispered.

"Excuse me?"

He put his hand on my shoulder and smiled again. People thought it was hard to be good, he explained, but they were wrong, dead wrong. "Oh, you can be bad all right—for a while. But you can't keep it up! It's just too damn hard! You always end up being good again!"

He squeezed my shoulder and chuckled as I got out. At the end of the drive, he gave a little toot. Then he was gone.

I turned to the house. My mother's light was on, and I pictured her lying in bed reading and smoking. And suddenly, right then and there, I felt that membrane tearing away, all the way off, and I was falling through to the other side. I thought about Angela Tourtelotte's question. No, I would *never* be happy, I decided, never in my life. For me, being unhappy was a calling, it was like the priesthood or like the bad breath some people have, you can cover it up but you can't get rid of it. I remembered how my mother used to take me down to the beach when I was a kid to watch the submarines, and one day we saw a sub going out with all the men on deck—and suddenly I was terrified my father was there, and he was going to drown, and I screamed and cried until my mother shook me and said, *Hey! Dad is sitting at his desk, right now, on dry land, honey!* That was how it went with me: Every single happy thing had some twist in it, some moment where it started to go bad.

I went inside, locked up, and went to bed.

The last two weeks of school everyone else was going wild, but all I wanted to do was sleep. In the middle of the night I'd come downstairs and eat. Then in the morning my mother would bang on the door. "Is the Snooze King grac-ing the court with his presence today?" she'd say.

At school I avoided Angela Tourtelotte. She followed me around, sulking. *Why are you harshing on me?* she kept saying. *What did I do?*

"Nothing," I told her. "I'm just hibernating, OK?"

She had a friend, Teddi, who kept giving me sinister lit-tle messages in the hall, like "You know, if you don't treat Angela right, you could *lose* her!" The two of them fol-lowed me around. It was like in a detective movie—I'd stop, they'd stop. At the water fountain I went to take a drink, and when I bent over there they were, huddling together.

"This is ridiculous," I said, standing up.

Teddi came over. "Angela isn't talking to you," she said.

"What are you," I said, "her bodyguard?"

"She's like, totally disappointed in you, you know."

Teddi's one of these people who wears pointy black glasses with fake diamonds in them and thinks it's cool. "If you'll excuse me," I said, "I was going to get a drink of water."

I bent over the fountain. "OK," Angela T called. "Let's *be* boring!"

I turned and faced her. "Do you realize you say the same things over and over again?" I said. "You have these three expressions. 'Let's *be* boring!' 'Go-carts *rule!*' 'Stop *harsh-ing* on me, Wally!' That's it—that's your whole vocabu-lary!" I turned and went down the hall.

"You are like, so lame, it's pathetic!" she shouted after me. "Go *be* alone, see what I care, you big . . . LUMP!"

I kept on walking.

After school that day I rode my bike down by the beaches. The streets were so familiar it felt almost sore rid-ing down them, that comfortable soreness like around the edges of a scab when you pick at it. I parked my bike and sat on the hurricane wall. An old man was flying a kite with his grandson, but there wasn't enough wind. He'd run a few steps and the kite would bob up, then sink down again. I thought about Montana and how far away it was. States out there were huge, their lines perfectly straight. The towns had names like Pierre and Helena. When it snowed, they got four feet, and the snow never got dirty; it just stayed there, shining white.

On Thursday before graduation we had rehearsal after school in the gym. First we got plastic packets with our gowns inside. Then the vice-principal, Mr. Eckert, explained how to get your diploma: Take with your left, shake with your right, and keep moving. Pierre Shavers, our senior class president, practiced his ridiculous speech. "All right" he shouted. "It's been wild, it's been real, party hearty, dudes!"

Afterward I sat until everyone was gone and the janitor, Fred, started folding up the bleachers. I liked how they folded and unfolded, creating hundreds of seats out of nothing, then taking them back again.

Someone coughed behind me. It was Angela Tourtelotte, standing by the door. Since our fight we hadn't talked. I went over.

"What, no bodyguard today?" I asked her.

"Hah hah." She was holding something wrapped in comic-strip paper. She handed it to me. "Here. It's not like you deserve this or anything, but. . . ."

I unwrapped the paper. It was a pair of bowling shoes. Plus a can of the disinfectant they spray when you turn them in.

"Thanks." I stared at the shoes. The truth was, I'd missed Angela Tourtelotte, but I didn't know how to say it. So I just stood there.

"Hey," she said. "Wanna go get scenic? I happen to know a *lovely* spot I could show you."

She held out her arm for me to take.

*   *   *

We walked over to Beaufort College, this junior college near school, and sat out in front of the student center. People were already gone for the summer, the campus was practically deserted. Every now and then someone would come out of the building and head across toward the library, carrying books or a briefcase.

"I wonder what I'm going to do," I said.

Angela looked at me. "You're going to go inside and get me a Coke."

I looked across the lawns. There was a little breeze, and the trees overhead rustled. Angela rolled the sleeves of her shirt up to the shoulders. Everything stood still.

"The leaves," I said.

"Huh?"

"You asked when was I ever happy. Well, I was happy when my sister used to throw me in the leaves. Out in the back yard. We used to rake leaves—"

"Rewind, rewind!" Angela Tourtelotte held her hands up. "*Sister?*"

And so I told her everything I hadn't told her— about Janice, about my mother and the red ribbons, Montana and the mountain in the sunshine: it all came flying out. And the leaves. I hadn't remembered those leaves until just then. We'd rake them up in the back, a giant mountain of leaves, and Janice would swing me around and then let me go and I'd float into the crackly pile.

When I was done, Angela picked a blade of grass and twirled it around. She shook her head. "Life is so weird. It's so, like, secret, you know?"

I waited. I guess I was expecting her to make some comment about Janice, but instead she proceeded to tell me about how her father had blatantly cheated on her mother three years before, how he'd bought his girlfriend a Mustang convertible, and how, after he finally got guilty and bagged her, the girlfriend traded the car in for lottery tickets—and won two hundred thousand dollars.

I stared at her.

"It's true! Right now she's on this island in Indonesia somewhere with a personal slave giving her total body massages."

Whatever the point was supposed to be, I didn't feel like getting it. We sat there. Angela Tourtelotte started doing the blade of grass routine again.

"You like it this way, don't you," she finally said.

"What way?"

"You know, the whole dead sister situation. The whole Montana thing. You're into it."

I just looked at her.

"That's right, you're into it. You're into it because it's, like, so impossible and perfect. It's so *done*. That's what you want to be. Totally done."

"Done?" I said. "What am I, a steak?"

She twirled the piece of grass, intensely staring at it. Then she flicked it away.

"Your sister could be anywhere, you know." She pointed to a girl in a jeans jacket sitting on a bench reading. "She could be her. Or she could be, like, a taxi driver somewhere. Or she could be one of them." The door to the student center had just opened and two women in cafeteria outfits were standing outside talking.

"Yup," Angela Tourtelotte said. "I think that one's definitely her. The tall one. That's Janice."

"You are very strange," I said.

"Just check it out," she insisted. "Just try to imagine it."

I watched as the woman reached into her purse and took out a cigarette. She had dyed reddish-brownish curled hair. She was at least fifty. Angela went on. "Maybe Janice has kids. Maybe she has twins, like Ricky and Mickey. Maybe triplets—you know, three pink little screamers. What do you think about that?"

"Who knows?" I said.

She reached over and grabbed my arm.

"Hey, I love you," she said. "What do you think about *that?*"

She let go of my arm and looked at me. I couldn't look back—I wasn't upset, I just couldn't look at her—so I closed my eyes and pretended to be enjoying the sun on my face. After a minute I really did start enjoying it. When I thought about it, it *was* funny to imagine Janice underneath the same sun somewhere, a waitress smoking a cigarette and boasting about her kids, bitching about taxes, telling someone how to make a killer avocado dip.

I opened my eyes. Angela Tourtelotte was standing up.

"Come on," she said. "Time to get scenic."

As it turned out, the spot she wanted to show me was the college greenhouse, way across campus. It was locked when we got there, and so we walked around, looking in. Angela started naming all the plants: snapdragons and coleus, Dusty Miller, sago palm. She and her mother, it turned out, did garden club together.

"Do a lot with sago palms in garden club?" I asked her.

"Oh you're so *funny*, it's hysterical!" She did an exaggerated nasal-drip laugh. Then she looked around and grabbed my hand. There was a little tool shed right by the greenhouse, and the door stood partway open.

Inside was dark and cool, with one tiny streaky window. My eyes adjusted and I saw shovels against the wall, trowels like claws, big bags of wood chips. I took an old chair and wedged it under the doorknob.

"My hero," Angela Tourtelotte said.

She was standing right in front of me, so close I could feel her breath on my chin. Her lips looked purple and shiny in the dim light—they *were* purple and shiny, I remembered.

"Hey," she said, "do you think I'm a sexy mama?"
Someone in the library had written *Angela is a Sexy
Mama* in the last carrel, she explained. She was hoping
maybe it was me.

*Me, a vandal*—? I started to say, and then she kissed me.
We rolled over on the bags of wood chips.

After a while I had to stop. "What's wrong?" she asked.

"I don't know how to say this, but . . . " I put on my AM-
radio voice. "I think I'm in the grip of the sexual urge."

"Ooo, dangerous!"

"No, seriously. Listen, uh, I've never actually, you
know—"

"God, you make it sound like we're *doing* it or something. I mean, this is just, like, cuddling." She kissed me.

"Hey. If we keep cuddling like this, I'm gonna explode."

"Don't worry, silly," she said. "I'll put you back together
again."

We rolled over, and a lot of things happened at once:
Angela slid her tongue into my ear, and I shivered; a
shadow crossed outside the window and then the door was
rattling and Angela was whispering *Shhhh!* as someone
outside croakily said, "What's going on in there? You OK
in there?"

Through the window I could see the shoulder of a campus security uniform. The door rattled again.

"We're just fine!" Angela called out. And the two of us
held on tight and did the nasal drip together, looking out at
the greenhouse and the sago palm, laughing like idiots in
the dark.

# Nobody Listens
# When I Talk

ANNETTE SANFORD

Locate me in a swing. Metal, porch type, upholstered in orange-striped canvas by my mother. I am spending the summer, my sixteenth, but the first I have spent in a swing. I could say I'm here because I have a broken leg (it's true I do have pain) or ear trouble or a very strict father. I could say I like to be alone, that I'm cultivating my mind, that I'm meditating on the state of the universe. I could say a lot of things, but nobody listens when I talk, so I don't. Talk. Not often, anyway. And it worries people.

My mother, for instance. She hovers. She lights in a wicker chair by the banister and stares at me periodically. She wears a blue-checked housedress or a green one under the apron I gave her for Christmas with purple rickrack on the hem. She clutches dust-cloth or a broom handle or the women's section of the *Windsor Chronicle*.

"Marilyn," she says, "a girl your age should be up and doing things."

Doing things, to her, is sweeping out the garage or mending all my underwear. Doing things, to me, is swimming, hanging on the back of a motorcycle, water-skiing. To her, a girl my age is an apprentice woman in training for three meals a day served on time and shiny kitchen linoleum, but she would be happy to see me dancing the funky-chicken if it would get me on my feet.

I stay prone. I don't want to do her kind of thing, and I

can't do mine. The fact is, I don't fit anywhere right now. Except in a swing. So here I am, reading.

My father arrives in the evening. He has worked all day in an office where the air conditioning is broken, or with a client who decides at five minutes to five to invest with another company. He flops in the wicker chair and communes with my mother's ghost.

"Marilyn," he says, "a pretty girl like you ought to realize how lucky she is."

Lucky, to him, is being sixteen with nothing to worry about. My father grew up in Utopia, where everyone between two and twenty dwelt in perpetual joy. If he were sixteen now he would have a motorcycle and a beautiful girl riding behind him. But it wouldn't be me. If he were sixteen and not my father, he wouldn't look at me twice.

From time to time my friend comes. I give her half the swing and she sits like a guru and pops her gum. She can do that and still look great. When she blinks, boys fall dead.

"Marilyn," she says, "a girl like you needs a lot of experience with different men."

She will get me a date with her cousin. With her sister-in-law's brother. With the preacher's nephew from Syracuse. She will fix me up in the back seat of the car with someone like myself, and we will eat popcorn and watch the drive-in movie and wish it were time to go home.

I could say, *I'm not that kind of girl at all.* I could say, *Someone should be kissing me madly, buying me violets, throwing himself in front of Amtrak for want of my careless glance.*

Who would listen?

So I say, "No." I say, "Maybe next week." Then I lie in the swing and watch the stars come out and wonder why I didn't go.

When you lie in a swing all day, you remember a lot.

You close your eyes and listen to the locusts humming in the elm trees and you think of who you are.

You think of you at six, crying into a blue corduroy bedspread because your uncle has laughed at your elephant, which has no tusks. You have drawn it as a gift for him. You have never heard of tusks before.

You think of lying in the big iron bed at Grandpa's house, listening to the cistern water tapping on the stones outside the window, knowing you are safe because you are the baby and everybody loves you. You think of the dancing class grand ball when you are twelve in a pink dress with ribbons in your hair and a head taller than the boy who brought you. His mother has made a corsage for you, and when you dance it rubs against his nose. You pretend he pulls away because of this, but when you are sixteen lying in a swing, you know it was the scent of your own self-doubt mingling with the rose and lavender that sent you to the chairs waiting by the wall.

When you lie in a swing all day, you live in the world you read about. You drag a bare foot back and forth across the floor and hear the song the chains sing, but you aren't really you.

You are a woman standing by a table, reading a letter from a box of other letters. A dead man wrote them. His face, as young as yours, he has given to the baby sleeping by the window where the boats pass. He has dreamed his own death and written a passage from the Psalms: *His days are as grass, in the morning they flourish, in the evening they wither and are cut down.*

You are a father counting cracks in the sidewalk passing under your feet. You have waited a long time in a railroad station for a train carrying the child who walks beside you, who says, *My mother made me come even though I hate you.*

You are a girl, pregnant, alone in a car you have parked

on a country lane. You are kin to the brown cow chewing across the fence. *You are wet and sticky and blind, curled in the cow's stomach waiting for your birth.* You are sick in the ditch.

You are a boy in a room with bars on the window, an old woman on white sheets looking at the Good Shepherd trapped in a frame, a child with a scar on his face.

When you aren't really you, then the who that you are is different somehow: strong, and part of everything... sure of a harvest every season... glad to be sad. You are a riddle with hundreds of answers, a song with a thousand tunes.

When you lie in a swing all summer, fall comes before you notice. Suddenly elm leaves pave the street, and you have been seventeen for three days.

It is time to get up.

In the kitchen my mother is still in her apron, frying the supper steaks. I sit at the table and eat a grape. I could say, *Don't worry about the underwear. When the time comes, I can mend it. I can cook and clean a house and love a lonely daughter. I was watching all summer.*

Instead, I yawn, and she looks at me. "A whole summer," she says, and shakes her head.

In the den the weatherman is promising rain. I kiss the top of my father's head where the hair doesn't grow anymore and lay my cheek on his whiskers. I could say, *I really am, like you said, beautiful.*

"Try something light for a change," he says, and hands me the funnies. I curl on the couch and call my girlfriend. She tells me she has kissed a trumpet player. He has an incredible lip. She tells me bikinis are on sale, blond men get bald first, mud is good for the skin.

I could tell her, *Summer's over.* I could say, *Men are born and die and are born again. The rest is only details.* I could say,

Roses are red,
violets are blue.
I grew up,
*but nothing happened to you.*

I don't, though. It hurts too much. And besides, nobody listens when I talk.

Sometimes not even me.

# Saint Chola

### K. KVASHAY-BOYLE

Skater. Hesher. Tagger.

Wanna-be. Dweeb. What-up.

Nerdy. Trendy. Freaky. In a few weeks it'll be solid like cement, but right now nobody knows yet. You might be anything. And here's an example: meet Mohammadee Sawy. Hyper-color t-shirt, oversize over-alls with just one hook fastened, the other tossed carefree over the shoulder like it's no big thing. In walks Mohammadee, short and plump and brown, done up for the first day with long fluffy hair and a new mood ring, but guess what, it's not *Mohammadee* anymore. Nope, because Dad's not signing you up today, you're all by yourself and when you get the form where it says Name, Grade, Homeroom, you look around and take the pen Ms. Yoshida hands you and you write it in big and permanent: Shala M. Sawy. And from now on that's who you are. Cool.

It's tough to do right, but at least you learn what to want. You walk the halls and you see what's there. I want her jeans, I want her triple pierce hoops, I want her strut, I want those boobs, I want that crowd, I want shoes like those shoes, I want a wallet chain, I want a baby-doll dress, I want safety-pins on my backpack, I want a necklace that says my name. Lipstick. I want lipstick. Jelly bracelets. Trainer bras from Target. It could be me. I could be anyone. KISS FM, POWER 106, Douche-bag, Horn-ball. Fanny packs!

Biker shorts! And suddenly, wow, Shala realizes that she has a surge of power inside that she never knew was there. Shala realizes that she's walking around and she's thinking, Yup, cool, or No way! Lame!

*Shala?* That sounds good. And that's just the way tiny Mrs. Furukawa says it in homeroom when she calls roll. She says *Shala.* And Shala Mohammadee Sawy? She smiles. (But not so much as to be uncool because she's totally cool.) And she checks out the scene. There's a powerhouse pack of scary Cholas conspiring in the back row. There's aisle after aisle of knobby, scrawny white-boy knees sprouting like weeds from marshmallow sneakers. And there are clumps of unlikely allies haphazardly united for the first time by the pride of patriotism: Serrania Avenue, row three; Walnut Elementary, row five; or MUS, first row. Forty faces. Shala knows some of them. Bad-ass. Gangster. Dork. Ido, Farah, Laura Leaper, Eden, Mori Leshum—oh great, and him: Taylor Bryans. Barf. But the rest? They're all new. So who knows.

In Our World, fourth period, you learn current events. It's social studies. The book's heavy. But then there's a war. And then you're embarrassed to say Niger River out loud, and you learn to recognize Kuwait, and a kid named Josh gets a part in a movie with Tom Hanks, but that's nothing you tell Lucy because you used to roller-skate at Skateland with the kid from *Terminator 2.* And he's cuter. Way cuter.

It's L. A. Unified, where there's every different kind of thing, but it's just junior high so you're just barely starting to get an idea of what it means to be some different kind of thing. There are piercings. There are cigarettes. Even drug-dealers. And with all that, there's the aura of danger all around, and you realize, for the first time, that you could get your ass kicked. You could get pounded after school, you could get jumped in the bathroom, you could get jacked-up, beat-up, messed-up, it's true, and the omnipresent possibility swells every exchange.

Mrs. Furukawa's new husband is in the army. She says so. She wears the highest heels you've ever seen a person wear. Her class reads *The Diary of Anne Frank*, but you know you're set, you already read it. Plus *A Wrinkle in Time*, and you read that one too. At home your mom says, Get out the flag, we want them to know what side we're on.

On television every night Bush says Sad-dum instead of Suhdom and your dad says it's a slap in the face. Your dad, the Mohammad Sawy from which your Mohammadee came, says it's on purpose, just to drive that bastard nuts. Your dad, sitting there in the saggy green couch, looks smaller than he used to, tired. You practice saying that big name both ways, first the real way and then the slap-his-face way.

Gym class is the worst because you have to get naked and that is the worst. Gym is what your friends feared most in fifth grade when you thought about junior high and you tried so hard to imagine what it would be like to be with other people and take your clothes off—(Take your clothes off? In front of people? Strangers-people? Oh yeah right. Get real. No way.)—and you started trying to think up the lie you'd have to tell your parents because they just wouldn't get it. A big important thing is Modesty. You know that. It's your cultural heritage, and naked is certainly not Modesty. On the first day just to be sure, you raise your hand and ask if you were a non-strip every day would you fail? And Ms. DeLuca says, Yes.

Some kids ditch but it's been three months. It's too late now. You're stuck with who you are by now and even though you're finally Shala you're still a goody-good, brainy dweeb. And dweebs just don't ditch. Not like you want to anyway. Except in Gym. That's when you do want to. You sit on the black asphalt during roll call with your gym shirt stretched over your knees so that it's still all bagged out twenty minutes later when the volleyball crashes bang into your unprotected head for the fifteenth time like it's been launched from some mystery rocket launcher and it's got a homing device aimed straight for you.

At twelve, no one knows anything yet, so what kind of name is Shala? Who can tell? And, plus, who'd even consider the question if parents didn't ask it? Sometimes kids slip up to you in the crush of the lunch line and speak quick Spanish and expect you to answer. Sometimes kids crack jokes in Farsi and then shoot you a sly glance just before the punch line. Sometimes you laugh for them anyway. Sometimes you'll try and answer, *Sí*, and disguise that Anglo-accent the best you can. *Sí, claro.* But the best is when a sleepover sucks and you want to go home and you call up your mom and mumble Urdu into the telephone and no one knows when you tell your mom, I hate these girls and I want to leave.

On Tuesday a kid wears a t-shirt to school and it says NUKE EM and when Mrs. Furukawa sees it, she's pissed, and she makes him go to the office, and when he comes back, he's wearing it inside out. If you already saw it, you can still kind of tell though. ME EKUN.

After school that day your cousin asks if you want to try Girl Scouts with her. Then she gets sick and makes you go alone. When you get there, it's totally weird for two reasons. First, your cousin's older by one year and she already wears a hijab, and when you went over to get her, she dressed you up. So now you're wearing a hijab and lipstick and your cousin's shirt, which says "Chill Out." Uncool. But what could you say? She's all sick and she kept cracking up whenever you put something else of hers on, and she's so bossy all the time, and then before you knew it the carpool's honking outside and your aunt shouts that you have to go right now. So you do. Then, second of all, you don't know anybody there. They're all seventh graders. It sucks.

They're baking banana-nut bread and the girl who gave you a ride says that you smell funny. What's worse than smelling funny? The first thing you do is you go to the bathroom and wash your hands. Then you rinse out your mouth. You try to keep the lipstick from smearing all over the place. You sniff your armpits. As far as you can tell, it seems normal. In the mirror you look so much older with Aslana's hijab pinned underneath your chin like that.

When you walk out of the bathroom you bump into the Girl-Scout-mom and almost immediately she starts to yell at you like you spilled something on the carpet.

Um, excuse me but this is a feminist household and hello? Honey, that's degrading, she says.

She must be confused. At first you wonder, Is she really talking to me? and like in a television sitcom, you turn around to check if there's someone else standing behind you.

Don't you know this is America, sweetheart? I mean have you heard of this thing feminism?

Yeah I'm one too, you say, because you learned about it in school and it means equality between the sexes and that's a good idea.

That's sweet. She looks at you. But get that thing off your head first, she says. You know you don't have to wear it. Not here. No one's gonna arrest you. I didn't call the police or anything, honey—what's your name?

The Girl-Scout-mom shakes her Girl-Scout-head and she's wearing a giant Girl-Scout outfit that fits her. She looks weird. Like an enormous kid, super-sized like French fries. You can just be yourself at our house, honey, she assures you. You can. What, your mom wears that? She's forced to? Right? Look at you. Well you don't have to, you hear me? Here, you want to take it off? Here, com'ere, honey.

And when you do, she helps you, and then after, you're ashamed that you let her touch it. Then you mix the banana-nut dough and you think it looks like throw-up, and that same girl says that you still smell like a restaurant she doesn't like. You really, really want to leave. Maybe if you stand still, you think, no one will notice you. On the wall there's a picture of dogs playing cards. Your cousin's hijab is in your backpack and you hold your whole self still and imagine time flowing away like milk down your throat until it's gone and you can leave.

There are scud missiles, yeah, but in sixth grade at LAUSD, there are more important things. Like French kisses. There's this girl who claims she did one. You just have to think, What would that be? because no one would ever kiss you. At least until you're married. Lucy Chang says it's skeevy anyway. Lucy Chang is your best friend. You tell her about Girl Scouts and she says Girl Scouts is lame.

On the way home from school you get knocked down by a car. With a group of kids. It's not that bad, kind of just a scary bump, from the guy doing a California-stop, which means rolling through the stop sign. At first he says sorry and you say it's okay. But when you suck up all your might and ask to write down his license plate number, he says no. You're dad must be a lawyer, he says, is that it? What, look, you're not even hurt, okay? Just go home.

You have some friends with you. You guys were talking about how you could totally be models for a United Benneton ad if someone just took a picture of you guys right now. You're on your way to Tommy's Snack Shack for curly fries and an Orange Julius. Uhh, I think we should probably just go, all right, Noel says, It's not that bad so we should just go.

Yeah, go, the man says. Don't be a brat, he says, Just go.

Okay fine, you say, fine I'll go, but FIRST I'm gonna write it down.

He's tall and he looks toward the ground to look at you. Just mind your own business, kid, she doesn't want you to. No one wants you to, he says.

Well I'm gonna, you say.

Look, you're not hurt, nobody's hurt, what do you need to for?

Just in case, you say. If it scares him, you're happy. You're in junior high. You know what to do. Stand your ground. Make your face impassive. You are made of stone. You repeat it more slowly just to see if it freaks him out. *Just. In. Case*, you say and you're twelve and if you're a brat then wear it like a badge.

At mosque there's a broken window. It's a disgrace, your father says, Shala, I tell you it's a damn disgrace. The hole in the window looks jagged like a fragile star sprouting sharp new points. It lets all the outside noise in when everybody's trying to pray, and cars rush past grinding their brakes.

There's a report in Language Skills due Monday and you have to have a thesis, so on the way home from mosque your mom helps you think of one. Yours is that if you were living in Nazi times, you would have saved Anne Frank. Your mom says that's not a thesis. Hers is that empathy and tolerance are essential teachings in every religion. You settle for a compromise: Because of Anne Frank's tolerance, she should be officially granted Sainthood.

At home, while your mom makes dinner, she stands over the stove as you peel the mutant-looking ginger root and there are lots of phone calls from lots of relatives. What are we going to do? your mom keeps demanding each time she talks into the phone, What? Tell me. What are we going to do?

Saddam does something. You know it because there are television reports. Everyone's worried for your older brother. He's studying in Pakistan with some friends and if he leaves now then he'll be out one whole semester because his final tests aren't for two more months. He's big news at the mosque. Also people are talking about the price of gas and how much it costs just to drive downtown.

Then Bush does something back, and the phone cord stretches as your mom marches over and snaps the TV off like she's smashed a spider.

The ginger and the asafetida and the mustard seed sauté for a long time until they boil down and then it is the usual moment for adding in the spinach and the potato and the oil, but instead the moment comes and goes and the saag aloo burns for the first time that you can remember and the delicate smell of scorched spice swirls up through the room as you watch your mom demand her quite angry Urdu into the receiver, and you realize that she doesn't even notice.

You know why she's upset. It's because everyone can tell Ahmad's American and he can't disguise it. He smells American, he smiles American, and his t-shirts say *Just Do It*, like a dare. And lots of people hate America. Plus, in that country, in general in that country, it's much more danger-ous. Even just every time you visit, you swallow giant pills, and still your weak sterile body gets every cold and all the diarrhea and all the fevers that India has to offer. It's because of the antiseptic lifestyle, your mother insists, Too clean.

In Science class, fifth period, you learn that everything is made out of stardust from billions of years ago. Instead of it being as romantic as Mr. Kane seems to think it is, you think that pervasive dust feels sinister. You know what happened to Anne Frank, and you can't believe that when she died she turned back into people dust, all mixed up with every other kind of dust. Just piles and piles of dust. And all of it new.

There are plenty of other Muslim kids. Tons of them at school. Everyone's a little freaked out. In the hall, after Science, you see an eighth grader get tripped on purpose and the kid who did it shouts, Send Saddam after me, MoFo, and he'll get whupped, too!

After school that day, at Mori Leshum's house, everyone plays a game called Girl Talk, which is like Risk, except it takes place at the mall. It gets old fast. Next: crank calls! One Eight-hundred Survival is 1, 8, 0, 0, 7, 8, 7, 8, 4, 8, 2, 5. Uh hi, I just got in a car accident and OH, OH, ME SO HORNY! You laugh and laugh but when it comes time for your turn to squeal breathy oinks into the phone the way you've heard in movies, you chicken out and everyone concludes that oh my god you're such a prude. Well at least I'm not a total perv, you say. Oi, oi, oh! Wooo! Ahh! moans Jackie, and when Mori's shriveled grandma comes in the room to get you guys pizza, you all shut up fast for one quick second and then burst into hilarity. The grandma laughs right back at you and she has a dusty tattoo on her arm, and it's not until years later that you realize what it is. Oh that, says Mori, It's just her boyfriend's phone number. She says she put it there so she won't get it lost.

Some things that you see you can't forget. On your dad's desk in his office where you're not supposed to touch anything, you see a book called *Vietnam*, and it's as thick as a dictionary and it has a glossy green cover. At random you open it up and flip. In the middle of a sentence is something about sex so you start to read quick. And then you wish you didn't. You slam it shut. You creep out of the office. You close your eyes and imagine anything else, and for a second the shattered starshape of your mosque window flashes to the rescue and you cling tight and you wish on it and you wish that you hadn't read anything at all. *Please*, you think, and you try to push the devastation shoved out through the sharp hole the same way you try to push out the sound of horns and shouts when you say prayer. *Please*, you think, but it doesn't work and nothing swoops in to rescue you.

Sex Ed is only one quarter so that for kids like you, whose parents won't sign the release form, you don't miss much. Instead of switching mid-semester, you take the biology unit twice and you become a bit of an expert on seed germination. Lucy tells you everything anyway. Boys get wet dreams and girls get cramps, what's that all about? she says. You look at her handouts of enormous outlined fallopian tubes and it just sort of looks like the snout of a cow's face and you don't see what the big deal is. You do ask, though, Is there a way to make your boobs grow? And Lucy says that Jackie already asked and No, there isn't. Too bad. Then Lucy says, I must, I must, I must increase my bust! And then you call her a Horndog and she calls you a Major Skank and then you both bust up laughing.

When it happens it happens in the stall at McDonald's. Paula Abdul is tinny on the loudspeaker. Lucy's mom asks what kind of hamburger you want and you say you don't eat this meat, it has to be fish fillet, please. With sweet-and-sour sauce, please. Then Lucy shouts, Groady, and you say, Bite me, and then you and Lucy go off to the bathroom together and while she's talking to you about the kinds of jeans that Bongo makes, and every different color that there is, and how if you got scrunchies to match, wouldn't that be cool? you're in the stall and you realize it like a loose tooth. Lucy, oh my god, Lucy, check this out, wow! It happened!

Are you serious, she says, Are you serious? Oh my god, are you sure?

I'm sure, you say, and you breathe in big chalky breaths that stink of bathroom handsoap, powdered pink. When you guys come back to the table and you eat your meal, it seems like a whole different thing being in the world. And it is.

That night you ask your mom if you can stay home from school on account of the occasion. She doesn't let you. She does ask you if you want to try her hijab on, though, and you don't tell her about Aslana's. Shala, she says, Shala, I don't know about right now. This just may not be the time. But it has to be your choice. You don't have to if you don't want to, but you do have to ask yourself how do you represent yourself now as a Muslim woman in this country, where they think that Muslims are not like you, Shala, and when you choose this, Shala, you are showing them that they know you and that you are nice and that you are no crazy, no religious nut. You are only you, and that is a very brave thing to show the world.

Now when you guys walk home, you're way more careful about not trusting any cars to do anything you expect them to. When you get to the 7-Eleven, you try different ways of scamming a five-finger-discount on the Slurpees. The woman behind the counter hates kids. Timing is everything. Here's how it goes: one person buys and you mix every color all together and try to pass from mouth to mouth and suck it gone before it melts. It's hard because of brain freeze. You try to re-fill and pass off, which the woman says counts as stealing and is not allowed, but that's only when she catches you. Trick is, you have to look like you're alone when you buy the cup or she'll be on to you and then she'll turn around and watch the machine. So everyone else has to stand outside with the bum named Larry and then go in one by one and sit on the floor reading trashy magazines about eye shadow while the buyer waits in line. Today that's you. You wait in line. You've got the collective seventy-nine cents in your hand. You freeze your face still into a mask of passivity and innocence.

As the trapped hotdogs roll over sweating on their metal coils, you hear the two men in front of you discussing politics and waiting with their own single flavor Slurpees already filled to the brim and ready to be paid for in full.

Same goddamn ground war we had in 'Nam, and hell knows nobody wants to see their baby home in a body bag. Hey.

The way I see it is, you got two choices, right? Nuke the towel-heads, use your small bombs, ask your questions later, or what you do is convert.

With you on the first one, buddy.

No, no listen: *convert*. Hell yeah, whole country. To Islam. To mighty Allah.

Aw, dude, what: you and the rag-heads?

But I got a point, right? Right? 'Cause what'd you think these bastards want? Right? Oh yeah, hey uh, pack of Lucky Strikes, huh? And how 'bout Superlotto? Yeah, one of those, thanks.

Next: you. You try to gauge how much this straggly woman sees. Can she tell? Muslim? Mexican? Does she know that your clothes are Trendy, that your grades are Dweeby, that your heart is Goodygoodie? Your face: unreadable, innocent, frozen. One Slurpee. Please.

You walk around the counter and toward the magazines and when your friends see you, you try to look triumphant and cool and with it. But you feel like a cheat. Like maybe if it is stealing, you might not be such a good Muslim, you might be letting your kind of people look bad.

Not *stealing*, says Lucy. Sharing. It's just sharing.

So you share. You slurp cherry-cola-blueberry-cherry layers until your forehead aches. Then Jackie opens up her mouth and throws her head back and gets down on her knees and another girl pulls the knob and you all stop to watch the Slurpee slurped straight from the machine. Gross, someone says, but you're all impressed with the inventiveness and Jackie's daredevil status is elevated in everyone's eyes.

Oh, give me a break! You damn good-for-nothing kids, get out of here! Get! Never again! You're banned, you hear me? Banned! Out! Get out!

Scatter giggling and shrieking across the parking lot, and the very next day dare each other to go back like nothing happened, and you know you can because you know she can't tell the difference between any of you anyway. You could be anyone, for all she knows.

The day you try it out as a test, someone yanks hard from behind and when it gets ripped off your head, a lot of hair does too. You think about how when hard-ass what-up girls fight they both stop first and take out all their earrings. It hurts enough to make you cry but you try hard not to. *Please don't let me cry, please, please don't let me cry.* First period, and Taylor Bryans sees your chubby lower lip tremble and he remembers the time you corrected his wrong answer in front of the whole class (Not pods! *Seeds*! Duh!) and he starts up a tough game of Shala-Snot-Germs which is so lame, but still the cooties spread from hand to hand all around the room as your face gets hotter and hotter and your eyeballs sting and your nose drips in sorrow. Your dignity gathers and mounts as you readjust the scarf and re-pin the pin. You can't see anyone pass Germs, you can't hear anyone say your name. You are stone. You are cool. You will not cry. Those are not tears. The bell rings.

Then the bell rings six more times at the end of six periods and when you get home that day you have had the hijab yanked on seven occasions, four times in first period, and you've had your feet stomped twice by Taylor Bryans in the lunch line, and after school, a group of eighth graders—all of them past puberty and huge with breasts in bras—surrounded you to gawk and tug in unison. And you've made up your mind about the hijab. It stays. No matter what. The fury coils in your veins like rattlesnake lava, the chin pushes out to be held high, the face is composed and impervious and a new dignity is born outraged where there used to be just Shala's self-doubt. It stays, you think, No matter what.

Still, at home you cry into your mom's sari and you shout at her like she's one of the merciless. I'm just regular, you wail. I'm the same as I ever was!

Oh baby, come on, *bendi*, shhh, it's going to be okay, she says. And then your mom suggests that maybe right now might not be the right time to start wearing this. She assures you that you are okay either way, that you can just take it off and forget about it. She says all this, sure, but she wears hers knotted firmly underneath her own chin as she strokes your back with reassurance.

That night, before you get into bed, you think about your brother and what it must be like for him. You look in the bathroom mirror and you slip the hijab on over your young hair and you watch like magic as you're transformed into a woman right before your very eyes. You watch like magic as all of the responsibilities and roles shift and focus.

You get it both ways. In your own country you have to worry, you have to get your hair pulled. And in India, there you are: the open target, so obvious with your smooth American feet and your mini Nike backpack, the most hated. With anger and envy and danger all around you. The most hated. The most spoiled. An easy mark. A tiny girl. With every thing in the world, and all of it at your disposal.

You think about your brother and you wonder if he's scared.

As you get dressed for bed you check things out with a hand mirror. You poke at the new places you hadn't looked at before. You look at the shape in the hand mirror and you think, *Hello me.* It's embarrassing even though it's only you. You feel a whole new feeling. You think about how much you hate Taylor Bryans. Indignation rises up like steam. You stand there in the bathroom with blood on your hands and you know it. *I am Muslim,* you think, *I am Muslim, hear me roar.*

In third period Gym, the waves of hot Valley sun bake off the blacktop asphalt and from a distance you see squiggly lines of air bent into mirage, and your head is cooking underneath the scarf and your ears feel like they're burning in the places where they touch the cloth and your hair is plastered to the back of your neck with sticky salty sweat, and when you group up for teams, someone yanks hard. You topple right over. You scrape your knees and, through the blood, they're smudged sooty black. Everyone turns around to look, and a bunch of girls laugh quietly behind hands. The hijab is torn from where the pin broke loose and your dad is right, it's way better that it isn't a knot or you might choke. Your neck is wet with a hair-strand of blood from where the popped-open pin tip slipped along skin. And you figure, That's it. Forget it. I quit. I'm ditching. I hate you.

Someone says, Aw damn, girl, you okay?

You scramble up and walk tall and leave the girls in their bagged out gym uniforms, and you go back into the cool dank locker room where you can get naked all by yourself for once. As you wash the gravel out of your hands, you stare at yourself in the mirror. You think, *Bloody Mary*, and squeeze your eyes shut tight, but when you open them it's still just your face all alone with rows and rows of lockers. No demon to slice you down.

Now when you walk in late you're not Nobody anymore, you're not Anyone At All. Instead, now, when you walk in, you have to brace yourself in advance, and you have to summon up a courage and a dignity that grows strong when your eyes go dull, and you stare into unfocused space inches away while Taylor Bryans and Fernando Cruz snicker and snicker until no one's looking, and then they run up and shout in your face: Arab! Lardass! Damn, you so ugly you ooogly!

Your inner reserves fill to full when Fernando stomps your feet, and your white Reeboks get smeared up and wrecked, and your face doesn't even move no matter how much it hurts.

The bell rings. Lunch. You push and shove your way into the cluster of the Girls' Room, and there's no privacy and you try to peer into the tagged-up piece of dull-shine metal that's bolted to the wall where everyone wants a mirror, but there are girls applying mascara and girls with lip-liner and the only air is a fine wet mist of aerosol Aqua-Net, and it's too hard to breathe, and you can't see if it's still pinned straight because that last snatch was like an afterthought and it didn't even tug all the way off. But you can't make your way up to the reflection and you can't see for sure. So here it comes, and then you're standing there in the ebb and flow of shoulders and sneakers, and all of a sudden here it comes and you're sobbing like you can't stop.

Hey girl, why you crying? Want me to kick some home-boy's ass for you, girl? 'Cause I'll do it, bitch, I'm crazy like that. You just show me who, right, hey I'll do it, yo.

And through your tears you want to throw your arms around the giant mountainous Chola and her bighearted kindness, and you want to kiss her Adidas, and you want to say Taylor Bryans' name, and you want to point him out, and you want his ass kicked hard, but you stop yourself. You picture the outcome, you picture the humiliation he'd feel, a skinny sixth grader, a scrub, the black eye, the dev-astation of public boy-tears, the horror of having someone who means it hit you like an avalanche. You look over your back, past all the girl-heads, the stiff blondes and permed browns and braided weaves, the dye jobs, the split ends, all of them elbowing and pushing in to catch a dull distorted glimpse in graffitied monochrome, and you smooth over the folds of your safe solid black hijab, and you snuffle up teary dripping snot, and you picture what it would be.

You picture her rush him: Hey BITCH, yah I'm talking to you, *pendejo*, that's right you better run outta my way whiteboy, cuz I'm going to whup your ass, you punkass bitch! You picture her and she's like a truck. Taylor Bryans stops cold and then he startles and turns to flee but she's already overcome him like a landslide, and she pounds him like muddy debris crushing someone's million-dollar home. You picture the defeat, the crowd of jeering kids, Fight! Fight! Fight! The tight circle of locked arms, elbow in elbow so the teachers can't break it up, the squawk of adult walkie-talkies and then the security guards, the assis-tant principal, and all the teachers on yard-duty, all of them as one, charging over to haul kids out of the fray and into detention, and all the while you can picture him like he's a photograph in your hand: the tears, the scrapes, the bruises, the giant shame in his guilty nasty eyes, and you know that it wouldn't solve a thing and you suspect that it probably wouldn't even stop him from pulling your hair out and stomping on your feet, and you picture it and you open up your heart and you forgive him.

Then you gather up all that new dignity, and then you look up at her, stick your covered head out of the girls' bathroom, and point.

# The Frontiers
# of Knowledge

CLAIRE ROBSON

My name is Timothy and I'm what you might call a "misogynist." If you don't know what that word means you should get a dictionary or put this story down and read something else. My father is a top army scientist. He has encouraged me to work hard and strive for academic excellence. Among other things, I have developed a very wide vocabulary, and I like to put it to good use. So there will be other difficult words. My father says that even though I'm only thirteen, my mastery of logic and my grasp of general knowledge surpass those of many of the adults who work for him in his department.

I don't like girls because they really are lightweight in terms of intellect. It's impossible to have a good discussion with them about interesting topics like computers, my first passion, or astronomy, which comes in second. Actually, no one at my school cares too much about anything serious. They are all too busy thinking about clothes and sex and television. But girls are the worst.

When I was younger, I used to think that I would become an army scientist, like my father, but now I think that computers are more important for the future of the world. Other than my father, a man who is at the head of his field, my other role model is Mr. William H. Gates. Mr. Gates is a ruthless entrepreneur. He's an example of Darwin's survival of the fittest. The liberal fringe says he's cold, but this is how Darwinism works. You have to have girls and women for the survival of the species, but mankind stays at the top of the food chain because people like Mr. Gates are pushing ahead the frontiers of knowledge. There will always be doubters when it comes to genius, but we can't let them stand in the way of progress.

My computer is top of the line. I won't tell you the specs because I'm constantly upgrading to the latest technology. I have about thirty different programs, including GPS, Astronomy Mapping, and a Net Sniffer, and many games (we don't even own a television). My favorite game is Victor, in which players compete online for world dominance. In Victor, terrorists have engineered a huge nuclear explosion that has wiped out most of Earth's population. This is sad, of course, but in another way it is not a bad thing, because the humans who are left have to pit their wits against each other in order to survive. When you play Victor, you have to tackle real world problems, such as food shortage and disease, and come up with real scientific answers. So Victor is extremely educational (as well as being a lot of fun). Every time you play, you face scientific problems that you have to research to find viable solutions. I do a lot of my research in the school library during recess.

The school library is supposed to be a quiet place where serious students such as myself can escape the stupid antics of all the rest and get on with something useful. But this is not always how it turns out. This one particular time, there was a group of girls sitting at a table next to me. They had some books out, but they didn't even pretend to look at them. They just sat there staring, like they'd never even seen a library before—which is probably true, come to think of it. In any case, this ended up with a lot of pushing and giggling and glances in my direction. Girls giggle a lot when they see me in the corridors, or in the lunchroom, a place I generally avoid. I suspect that this is because I am not what you would call "classically hot." I'm on the short side, though extremely wiry. (My father says that a healthy body is essential to intellectual superiority and so I work out on his Bowmaster twice a day.) Like many scientists, I wear glasses, and one of the girls in this group—all dyed hair and makeup—said something about how "four-eyed aliens" must have landed. Of course, her friends thought that this was very witty.

"Welcome to Planet Earth!" one of them called out to me. Then another one asked, "Greetings, Alien! How does your species reproduce?" —a question I did not dignify with a reply. I have found that it makes no sense to try to reason with people like this, and anyhow, they were all tangled up in a heap by this time, laughing hysterically.

"Who the hell dresses you?" the one with all the makeup said. "Your momma rush out to Goodwill every time they put up a Clearance sign?"

I don't have a mother, and I'm not interested in fashion, though of course it would have been futile to try to explain that to them. In Victor, everyone wears special jumpsuits that offer protection from the extremely high levels of radiation. Those girls in the library wouldn't have lasted a minute. They were inadequately dressed and mentally ill-equipped. In the end the librarian reprimanded them, but not before one of them had said some more unpleasant things, this time about my hair, which is naturally curly. The librarian, a woman, took way too long, in my opinion, to tell them to take their noise outside, which they finally did. Of course they just left all the books they'd been pretending to read on the table, plus candy wrappers and crumpled paper on the floor. It goes without saying.

After they left, I went back to reading *The Road Ahead* (which is a book written by Mr. Gates) when something else interrupted my train of thought. A shadow had fallen across the page where Mr. Gates was explaining how to wire the world. I looked up quickly, thinking the horrible girls had come back. And there was a girl, but only one, just standing there by herself, staring at me with her fingers wrapped together in a kind of knot and clutched to her chest.

"I saw the whole thing," she said, unwrapping her fingers and making a jerky little motion with her hands. "I was working at that table over there, or at least trying to, with all their noise."

"Yes. Well," I said, "I didn't really pay too much attention. 'Sticks and stones can break your bones, but words can never hurt you.'"

"But they were so mean . . . " she said. And for a second I thought she was going to cry, because her voice kind of faded off, and her face got pink. She had that pale kind of freckly skin and blond eyelashes that don't stand out very well, and glasses that made her eyes seem big and slippery.

I waited politely to see if she wanted something, although I was anxious to get back to reading *The Road Ahead*. After a fairly long pause, she asked what I was reading, so I held the book up so that she could see the cover, and—guess what? She'd already read it! We both laughed a little at that coincidence and it seemed to break the ice. It turned out that she was interested in computers, too. When I asked her what she had, though, she gave a big sigh and rolled her eyes and said her parents could only afford a 128 meg hand-me-down. I didn't point out that a lot of current applications wouldn't run on that kind of dinosaur. I guessed she already knew, since she seemed quite intelligent for a girl. Also, she was not bad looking. By that I don't mean that she wore tight clothes and too much makeup like those other stupid girls. She wore simple pants and a shirt and had her hair tied in a ribbon. She just looked ordinary and nice. To make a little conversation, I asked her if she knew that freckles like hers are caused by pigment cells. I happened to know that people with pale skin like hers have less melanin. This came as a complete surprise to her.

This girl's name was Helen, which is either from the Greek word *helene* meaning "torch" or the Greek word *selene,* which means "moon" (I did not know this at the time, but I looked it up when I got home). We talked for a while, and I ended up telling her about Victor. She asked a lot of questions. She even said that she would like to buy a copy, but I happened to know that it was no longer on sale. It hadn't done too well commercially. Most people just want games where they just get to shoot enemies and there is no intellectual challenge. Shooting is sometimes necessary in Victor, but ammunition is limited, so you have to weigh the pros and cons—not kid's stuff like in Quake where you find spare ammunition around every corner.

When I told her that she couldn't buy the game anywhere, she looked disappointed. I had an idea then. I asked her where she lived and when she said that she lived five blocks away on Sunny Street, I said, "If you come to my house this weekend and bring a CD I could burn a copy of Victor for you."

Helen hesitated, and I remembered that Sunny Street is where the poorer people live. Maybe her parents wouldn't let her buy too many CDs.

Part of being a good world leader is being sensitive to the needs of the people. This is called having "people skills." You start the game with only half a quota of people skills, but you can hone them and add to your quota as you go along. So I had become quite good at reading signals.

"Your dad will be there, right?" Helen asked.

"Probably not," I replied. "He's finishing up an important project right now, so he'll probably be in his office most of the weekend. But it doesn't matter. I know how to burn CDs. It's simple and I have plenty of blanks. My dad buys me whatever equipment I want. I just post a list of what I need on the bulletin board. We call it a note to central command!"

Here was another example of my people skills—making a little joke at my own expense. And it seemed to work, because she smiled a bit.

"How about your mother?" she asked then. "Will she be home?"

I don't like personal questions. "She's not in the picture," was all I said. "She's history."

This wasn't quite true—I do remember my mother—even though she left when I was only six years old. One thing I remember is how I would sit on her lap and she would smooth my hair flat with a wet brush. I still feel happy when I remember that—she is my own mother after all—but she was an alcoholic and not a fit parent and she stopped visiting a long time ago. My father says that she used to complain constantly about the long hours that he had to work on his special projects. It's true that he often does not get home until late, after I've gone to bed, but as I said before, it's the duty of family members to respect and support men like my father as they work to extend our knowledge of the known universe. After all, without people like them, what would happen to mankind?

Though I have learned to be self-reliant and am usually very happy with my own company, I became quite excited at the prospect of Helen's visit that coming Saturday. For the rest of that week, I limited my games of Victor to two hours a night, even though one of the other players (my arch enemy, Nemo) had circumvented the alarm system I installed around the perimeter of my enclave. I should really have tried to discover how he was doing that, but instead of playing until I heard my father come home late at night, I tried to clean up my room a little. My dad says that a man's room is his castle and he never interferes with mine, but when I thought of Helen coming, I suddenly realized that some of the clothes I had left lying around had started to smell like old things in a thrift shop, and that Coke had congealed in a lot of the glasses lying around and that there was mold on some of the plates. Penicillin has already been invented but I bet I would have invented it if it hadn't been.

By the time Saturday afternoon came along, when Helen had said she would arrive, my room was all cleaned up. I had even picked some flowers from the garden and put them in a little vase. The idea of the vase is something my mother used to do. When I was a little boy, I would sometimes pick violets from the lawn and bring them to her and she would arrange them, so I knew that this is something that girls like.

By one o'clock, with only an hour to go, I had become somewhat nervous. I don't often think about my personal appearance, but now I went into my dad's room and looked at myself in the mirror. I was wearing my normal uniform of black chinos (which Dad buys for me in bulk) and a plain t-shirt, which is the only type that I like to wear. I change my t-shirt and chinos when they look dirty, and these were still fairly clean, but I looked grungy somehow, and this was a big day. In between cleaning up and picking the flowers, I had gone online and not only thwarted Nemo's attack on my defenses, but figured out a way through his. We had been locked in combat for about eight weeks, and between us had killed off all our opposition. I was pretty confident that this would be the big showdown—the day that I would achieve world domination. So to celebrate, I took a shower and put on the suit and tie that I wear for visiting my grandmother. I even took a bottle of cologne from Dad's dresser and dabbed some on my chin. It felt like a special occasion.

When the doorbell rang, in my hurry to answer, I almost tripped coming down the stairs. That would be a joke! I thought to myself—to fall down the stairs and die! Wouldn't Nemo just love that! I was still smiling at the thought when I opened the door.

Helen looked nice. She had done something different to her hair, which was not tied back, but extra special curly, and she had on a pretty dress that was covered with ruffles. She held out a box of cookies. "My mother sent these."

We went upstairs and I showed her some of my things—my microscope and my telescope. She seemed impressed. I poured some Coke into clean glasses and booted up the computer. Though the counterattack was fully planned, I had not yet implemented it. I thought I would be nice to save it for Helen. I had become seriously hungry after all my preparations, so I ate tons of the cookies, which happened to be my favorite—double chocolate chip. I explained my plan of attack.

"We'll lure the soldiers out with a feint. A feint is where you pretend you're attacking, but it's not the real attack," I told her. "Watch."

I sent a small battalion of Troggs toward the entrance of Nemo's enclave—just enough to look convincing. We watched the alarm lights flashing on his main gate. It swung open, just as I had anticipated, and a stream of Nemo's own Troggs issued forth, ready to annihilate mine. I felt a great sense of satisfaction that my assessment of Nemo's personality had been accurate. He was somewhat impulsive.

Helen leaned forward. Her leg touched mine, accidentally, I thought, and I moved away, but not before I got goose bumps. "That's amazing," Helen said. She turned to me and her eyes were sparkling behind her glasses. The graphics on Victor are pretty impressive and I was sure she hadn't seen anything like this with the set up she has. Besides which, no one had ever really seen me in action as "Big Brill," which is my player name.

It was time for my piéce de resistance (that means the "main exhibit"). "Hit that button," I said, pointing. I leaned back in my chair a little, ready to enjoy the show.

"Why?" asked Helen. "What will happen?"

I was exasperated, though I didn't let it show. We had only a very tiny window of time to launch the rocket with the virus in the warhead. "Just press it," I told her. I was the one in charge here—the leader—and Helen was just a bystander really—but she was still staring at the screen with her forehead all scrunched.

"Who's inside the gate?" she asked.

"His tribe," I told her. "When the virus is launched, well, that's it. They'll all be wiped out. My Troggs will be infected too, but my tribe, all the women and children and the soldiers, are safe in their enclave. I've invented a serum for them. Nothing can touch them. And when my Troggs come back, if any do, my soldiers will execute them so that they can't infect us when the serum wears off. The virus dies after ten hours. That's the beauty of this scheme."

"That's horrible," she said, turning around to stare at me. "Why do the poor Troggs have to die, and Nemo's women and children?"

We were running out of time and I was getting angry. "It's called military expedience!" I told her. "You won't understand it! You don't need to understand anything! Just press the button! That's an order!"

When she didn't, I reached my hand out to press it myself, but she put hers out so that I couldn't reach and said, "Why are you being so mean?"

That's what I get for trying to help a girl. It was just like what happened with the Siege of Troy. All those heroes dead for one stupid woman. I stared at the screen as the gate started to swing shut behind Nemo's Troggs. They marched toward my enclave, and their gate closed behind them. The only way that I could have activated my own defenses was to have pushed Helen away from the controls, and my father had told me that whatever women did, I was never ever to raise my hand to them. Even when my mother did the worst things, he said, he had stuck to that principle.

I couldn't help it. When I watched the Troggs march straight through the main gate of my enclave, where no enemy had set foot before, I knew it was all over, and I started to cry. Leaders don't cry. I haven't cried since I was a child, since the day that my father told me that my mother wouldn't be coming to see me anymore. Worse, once I started I couldn't seem to stop. It was all that work, all that planning wasted, and Nemo striding about in my enclave, victorious, and his Troggs butchering everyone in sight—the women and children that I had taken care of and protected, my capable lieutenants and all my men. I put my head in my hands and sobbed for a long time.

I felt Helen's hand on my arm again. "I'm sorry," she said. "Can't we just start another game?"

I shook my head no. It was spoiled now, ruined. I knew that I would never play Victor again.

"It was only a game," she said. "Can't we start a new one? You could show me the right way to play." I felt her touch my hair.

That's when I got extremely angry. I didn't hit her, but I called her a lot of names—ones I'd heard my father use when he and my mother were fighting. I thought I had forgotten all those arguments—I was very young at the time—but some of the words came back, words he used to say to her when he was fed up. Many of the words I yelled at Helen were curse words, and when I thought about it later I wished I hadn't used them, because cursing is just a sign of a limited vocabulary and an inability to express yourself clearly. I was under extreme provocation, but, even so.

Helen left in a hurry, and she was crying, but I didn't feel sympathetic. It was all her fault and just typical of a girl. Women don't get the big picture, and that's why they are born to raise children and be nurturing, and why they should not be in the army, and why it's always men who should always have control of the button that could launch the missiles that could destroy the world.

# Gypsy Girl

## CAITLIN JEFFREY LONNING

Gypsy Girl Rule #1: *Never take candy from strangers.*

Gigi slid the money across the top of the counter, standing on tiptoe to see over it. She had always been "too small for her age," as her mother said. "One day you will sprout, Gigita, and be tall and beautiful, like all women in our family." Gigi thought that maybe she was just small, like her name. Her size and name had one other thing in common: she hated both.

"Pump five," she told the cashier, looking out at the RV parked in front of the gas station, its garishly painted sides drawing the attention of other customers in their cars. "Madam Vorinski's Fortune Telling" was painted in huge purple letters along one flank of the RV, next to a rough painting of a crystal ball. Gigi was used to the RV receiving strange looks, but maybe the people at the gas station were really staring at Gigi's mother, who was standing by the front of the RV, as straight and rigid as a pole and draped in the black mourning robes she'd worn for the eight years since Gigi's father died soon after Gigi's birth. Gigi's mother paid no attention to the small audience she had acquired—she just squinted straight ahead, through the clear glass front of the gas station, watching Gigi intently for any sign of trouble, the way she always did. "I must watch you this way, Gigita!" Mother exclaimed in her strange accent whenever Gigi complained. "What if one day I do not, and a man takes you from me? What then? We both die. Women like us cannot survive alone." Gigi doubted that any man would even consider stealing a scrawny runt like her away to anywhere, but her mother seemed convinced.

The cashier smiled warmly down at Gigi as she took her money and counted out the change. This woman looked so rooted where she was; as though she were a built-in fixture of the grungy gas station, bolted to the floor behind the chipped counter and in front of the shelves of cigarettes, her off-white hair and skin blending like camouflage with the off-white walls and shelves. She would never have to move or fear change. Change would never overtake the 7-Eleven cashier.

Gigi felt hollow, and must have looked that way because the woman reached down and pulled a candy bar from the rack in front of her counter.

"It's free, hon," she explained when Gigi began to protest. "You look like you could use some nourishment."

Gigi had never been given extra money in her life, especially not for frivolous things like candy, for which she had never felt much desire. Yet as she slowly peeled off the wrapper and examined the dark chocolate underneath, it was hard to imagine anything more wonderful.

Before she could take a bite, the shop's bell clanged angrily, as if in divine warning. A second later, Gigi's mother descended on her and snatched the bar out of her hand, looking like an avenging angel.

"How many times have I tell you, Gigi!" she shrieked, slamming the driver's side door of the RV and stamping on the gas pedal. "You never take gifts from strange women! Can you not see what she was? A *kehiyo*! She could have ripped out your liver and eat it for snack! You want that?"

Gigi's mother always spoke this way, and used words that no one else did, like *kehiyo*, which meant "witch." When she was younger, Gigi would imitate the accent and believe the words, thinking that her mother was from some far off, exotic country, where the people could recognize kehiyos as easy as breathing. Last year, Gigi found out that her mother was from central Ohio, the only state in the country they hadn't stayed in. Now Gigi wonders if perhaps her mother's fears of things like kehiyos and dangerous men are as fake as her accent and made-up words.

*Gypsy Girl Rule #2: Don't ever stop moving.*

Gigi's earliest memory was from when she was four, before she and her mother had even owned the painted RV. They'd lived in a tiny apartment in a big city. Gigi had friends, though she could no longer remember their names, and toys, though she could no longer picture them. She could remember a sense of contentment from her mother, something that now seemed as out of place on her as bright colors. Gigi could remember one other thing: a letter that had arrived late one fall afternoon. Gigi's mother looked at the envelope for a moment as she sorted through the mail. She set it aside, as if to read it later, but the next time Gigi saw it, the letter was crumpled and half buried in the soil of a potted plant. For a joke, Gigi thought she would take the letter from the plant pot and keep it in her room until she figured out how to give it back to her mother, who would be surprised that Gigi had been clever enough to find it.

The next morning, before the sun came all the way up, Gigi's mother was shaking her awake.

"Get on shoes," she had hissed in a hoarse whisper. "We are going."

Gigi hadn't had the sense to ask where they were going, or for how long. In retrospect she wished that she had; maybe it would have allowed her enough time to say good-bye to her home, her toys, and her friends, none of which she ever saw again.

"We must move always, Gigita!" her mother had said, hurrying her down the dirty street outside their apartment. "You stay too long and the demons catch up to you! They try to take you from me! And what then? We die. Women like us cannot survive alone."

*Gypsy Girl Rule #3: Beware of wily demons.*

The letter moved with them, although Gigi quickly forgot she had it. She found it again in the lining of her battered suitcase when she was eleven years old, and started to read.

> Dear Ms. Collins:
>
> The judgment of dissolution of marriage re: Lowenberg v. Lowenberg ordered shared custody of Georgia. Your unilateral removal of Georgia from the State of Ohio is in direct violation of the court's order. Furthermore, your failure to inform Mr. Lowenberg of Georgia's whereabouts calls into question your fitness as a parent.
>
> Be advised that the court has set down this matter for a full hearing on October 19, 1998 at nine o'clock in the forenoon at the courthouse at 783 Main St., Cincinnati, Ohio. On behalf of Mr. Lowenberg I intend to invoke the full contempt powers of the court and will seek a modification of the outstanding custody orders in order to provide full custody to Mr. Lowenberg.

Gigi stopped reading as the letter was wrenched from her hands, and she looked instead into the blazing eyes of her mother. Her mother looked at the letter and wailed loudly when she saw what it was. She burned the letter, proclaiming it an unworthy trick by wily demons. She spent several days after that in her cot in the RV with a cloth over her eyes and a bottle of amber liquid in her hand, and did not speak to her daughter for a week.

*Gypsy Girl Rule #4: Never dream.*

Gigi turned twelve, and her birthday went as unnoticed as the others before it. She didn't understand why birthdays were considered something to celebrate. It was just another year closer to death, another year of never stopping because of her mother's fear of demons, dangerous men, candy, and kehiyos. The list seemed to keep growing.

Lying in her ratty RV bed late at night and listening to her mother move bottles in the kitchenette, Gigi remembered the court letter from years before, straining her mind to recall exact words and phrases, and puzzling out the meanings. When Gigi had asked, Mother had only repeated that the message was left by demons, trying to trick them. "Your father is dead. Your name is Gigi, not 'Georgia'. The demons are no good at tricks—they do not even know us! Believe your mother, Gigita. Why would I lie about this?"

It was a question Gigi couldn't answer. Why would her mother lie about anything? It made no sense, but Gigi was almost certain she didn't believe in demons, and she could not believe that she and her mother were the only good people in the world.

One day she would live in a house like her old one, with friends and a car that only drove for a few miles at a time before it gave out and had to be taken back home for refueling. She'd be called Georgia by everyone, and she would find Mr. Lowenberg, if he was her father, and tell him that he could have all the custody he wanted.

Gigi rolled over in the dark and wrapped her arms around her stomach, trying to ignore the pain in it. She reminded herself of Rule #4. Somehow dreaming always made things seem worse.

*    *    *

*Gypsy Girl Rule #5: All other rules are void.*

Another state, another gas station late at night. Sixteen-year-old Gigi carefully counted out the coins needed to pay for the gas and lay them gently on the counter. This time, the cashier was a man, and he offered Gigi something other than candy.

Gigi looked out the glass front of the gas station at the painted RV, its colors dimmed by age and darkness. The purple words advertising Madam Vorinski's Fortune Telling had faded along with Gigi's mother's work; only the shadow of "Mad" remained. Gigi's mother didn't stand beside the RV watching her anymore; she was sleeping in the passenger seat, exhausted by the effects of alcohol. It was typical of her life, Gigi thought, that whenever she actually needed her mother, she wasn't there.

Gigi took her change, ignoring the cashier, and left the store. There were no jangling bells as the door opened, just the loud rumbling of a motorcycle pulling up in front of her. A tall, skinny boy climbed off and walked into the store. Like Gigi's mother, he wore all black, but the color looked different on him. On him it meant power. On Gigi's mother it just meant fear.

Gigi examined the bike. It was shiny and small, and only two colors. Gigi imagined the size of the gas tank. It couldn't be very large—the rider must have to stop often to refuel.

The thing that finally made up Gigi's mind was the license plate on the back of the bike. It had a ripe, fresh peach on it, and her name. *Georgia.*

When the boy came back out of the store, he saw a girl sitting on his motorcycle, watching him with dark eyes. She looked strange and wild, and he didn't ask her any questions.

As the boy started the bike, Gigi put her arms around his waist and smiled. This boy would call her Georgia.

# April

KATHARINE NOEL

Another windstorm had knocked out the farm's electricity, so the dining hall was lit by candles. In the three months she'd been here, they'd lost electricity three times. Angie liked how the flickering light made the movements of the Staff and Residents oddly holy, seeming to invest the smallest gesture—emptying a cup, unbuttoning a coat—with grace and purpose. In the candlelight, the tremor in her hands was barely visible. One of the things she hated about lithium was the way she shook, as though she were seventy instead of seventeen. This half-light meant she didn't have to pull her sleeves down over her hands or turn her body so that it was between other people and whatever she held. Angie didn't know what she was going to do about the trembling this afternoon, when Jess visited. Keep her hands in her pockets, maybe.

"Eggs and bacon," said Hannah, folding back the foil from a pan. She lifted the serving tongs. "What can I get you, Doug?"

"Yeah, yeah." Doug was sitting on his hands; his long legs knocked against the underside of the table.

"You want both?"

"Yeah." As he reached for his plate, a coin of scalp shone at the back of his hair where he'd begun to bald.

Hannah was Staff, one of the college students taking a

semester off to work at the farm. She'd told Angie that she would write a paper at the end and be given course credit by the Psych Department. Most of the college students looked biblical, with their long hair and rough shirts, but Hannah had crew-cut hair and overalls. She wasn't pretty, but she was graceful, and that, combined with her extreme thinness and short hair, made her stand out in a way the prettier students didn't.

She finished serving and closed the tinfoil back over the pans. Doug had already wolfed down half his food, and he held out his plate anxiously. "Can I have seconds now?"

"What's the rule, Doug?"

"Not until six-forty-five."

"Yeah, I don't think everyone's up yet."

Doug put his hands under his thighs again. He rocked forward. "I used to have a car. A Honda Civic. It was green. They're good cars, aren't they? Aren't they?"

"Damn good cars," Hannah said. Angie liked that Hannah talked to Residents, even the most floridly psychotic, about whatever they wanted to talk about. Most Staff insisted on reality-checking every two seconds.

The milkers came in, stamping snow from their boots. Sam Manning poured himself sap tea from the samovar. He had gray hair, cracked hands, wrists so wide he could have balanced his teacup on one of them. Sam was the only Resident who milked—the other milkers were on Staff— and so he'd been down to the barn already this morning. He sat down next to Angie. His boots gave off the sweet, murky smell of cow dung, and when he reached for the sugar bowl, she felt cold air on his sleeve.

"The big day," he said.

Angie nodded and looked away. With Jess's visit only a few hours away, thinking about it made her feel as though she had something sharp caught in her throat. They hadn't seen each other in the time Angie had been at the farm.

Sometimes Angie couldn't bring her memory of Jess's face into focus, which gave her the crazy fear they wouldn't recognize each other. At least the doctor had taken her off antipsychotics completely now. She was fat and she trembled, but each word wasn't its own search-and-rescue mission.

"They're good, they're good, they're good cars. They're good cars. They're *good cars*. Mine was green. Not too slow and not too fast. Not too safe and not too unsafe. Not *too* safe. Can I have more bacon?"

"She said six forty-five," a Resident said reprovingly.

"She said, she said, she said bedhead."

Hannah shrugged lightly. "About ten more minutes, Doug."

The door behind them opened, bringing the din of wind. Cold air rushed into the dining hall; the candle flames hunched low, wincing. The Residents who'd just come in had to struggle to close the door.

"Do you ever see any of your old friends?" Angie asked Sam. "From before you got sick?"

"Before I got sick was a long time ago."

"But do you?"

"I'm not like you." He turned his big hands over, looking neutrally at the dirty nails a moment before looking up at Angie again. "I've never been good with people. Really my only friend is my sister."

Angie still hadn't gotten used to the way people here said agonizing things so matter-of-factly. *He couldn't stay married to a mental patient. My mother says it would have been better I wasn't born.* Angie said, "You have lots of friends here. You have me."

"You were asking about outside, though. You're nervous about your friend coming."

"Not really," she lied. Jess had been her best friend since second grade. Up until the breakdown, they'd seen each other almost every day. Now when Jess called on the pay-phone, Angie sometimes whispered, "Tell her I'm not here."

Hannah yawned, covering her mouth with the back of one hand, blinking as her eyes watered. The yawn went on so long that she looked embarrassed by it. Gesturing toward the long table behind her, she said, "I've been up since four making bread. It's still hot, if anyone wants some."

"I fed on dead red bread, she said. She said, come to Club Meds in my head." Doug rocked forward, then back. "Is it lemon bread?"

"Just regular bread. Wheat bread."

Doug shook his head, making a face. He was too tall to sit at the table without hunching, and his knees hit against the underside, making the plates jump. "Sorry, sorry." He hunched even more. His scalp showed, waxy, through his thinning hair.

Nurse Dave had the med box. He poured pills into Doug's cupped palm: Klonopin, a green pill Angie didn't recognize, the same yellow and gray capsule of lithium she took three times a day. She looked away. Their movements were shadowed on the wall behind them, Nurse Dave straightening up, Doug remaining stooped as he reached for his water. The nurse watched Doug swallow his pills, then handed Angie her envelope, which she tucked beneath the edge of her plate. She'd only just gone from monitored to unmonitored meds, which meant no one watched her take them. She wanted to wait a few minutes, to make being unmonitored matter.

"An engine is a thing of beauty," Doug said.

A Resident said, "Here we go."

Hannah kept her voice casual. "What did you do last night, Doug? Did you watch the movie?"

"An engine is a thing of beauty, a thing, a thing, thing of *beauty*. Injector, *intake manifold* valve spring *timing* belt cam*shaft *inlet* valve com*bus*tion chamber *pis*ton skirt alternator *cool*ing fan *crank*shaft *fan* belt *oil* pan gasket oil *drain* plug oil *pan air* conditioner com*pressor*—"

Hannah glanced at the clock: it was only six-forty but she said, "Do you want some more bacon, Doug?"

"*Fly*wheel *en*gine block ex*haust* manifold exhaust *valve* spark plug *rocker* arm spark plug *cable* cylinder *head* cover vacuum diaphragm, distributor *cap*, in*jec*tor, *in*take manifold valve *spring*, timing *belt*, camshaft, *inlet* valve, com*bus*tion chamber, *pis*ton skirt *al*ternator *cool*ing fan crankshaft." When someone rose, his shadow—huge and flickering—leapt up and slid across the east wall, stooped as he scraped his plate, straightened to set the plate in the sink. Doug rocked forward in his chair. "Fan *belt* oil pan gasket oil drain plug oil pan air compressor—con*di*-*ti*oner—compressor flywheel engine block exhaust manifold. Inlet *valve*. Combustion *chamber. Piston.*"

At seven, they went in to Morning Meeting. Everyone wore jeans and work boots at the farm— Residents' usually newer and nicer, Staff's more likely to be worn and mended. Angie and Sam found seats together. Across from them, a Resident in a denim hat licked his chapped-to-bleeding lips, over and over. Staff whispered something to him and he stopped for a moment. Aside from the attendance sheets some the Resident Advisors balanced on their knees, Morning Meeting reminded Angie of Unitarian Church services she'd gone to with Jess: folding chairs, announcements, singing with guitars. To the east, against the mountains, the sky was purple with dawn.

They sang with heavy emphasis: Left a good *job* in the *ci*ty, working for the *Man* every *night* and day.

Some Staff were knitting, needles clicking softly. One of the biblical college students had taught Angie how, but she only knit where no one could see her—lithium worsened her natural clumsiness. It would be nice to have something to do with her hands, though. Sitting here gave too much room to think, so that Morning Meeting often turned into a half-hour meditation on ways she'd screwed up. The last time she'd gone to Jess's church she'd been awake for days. She gulped vodka in her room before church, trying to calm down, and the combination of mania and alcohol meant that she didn't remember much of the morning now. She did remember banners made of felt on felt—*joy, peace,* an abstract chalice. She remembered screaming with laughter at the stupid banners, she remembered during the service talking loudly to Jess, she remembered falling down after the service, suddenly surrounded by legs. The way noise was sucked out of the room. By her face was Jess's mother's ankle, stubbled with hair. The silence after her fall had probably only lasted a couple of seconds, but it had seemed much longer. She saw each black hair on Mrs. Salter's ankle sprouting sharp from its follicle, each follicle a pale lavender indent, and under the skin the hair continuing down, ghostly, toward its root. Above the anklebone was a small scar, white as a chalk mark. Angie could see Mrs. Salter in the shower, rushing a pink razor up her calf; the sharp, coppery taste that came into your mouth even before you consciously knew you were cut; the way that the area around the cut would have flinched back, and then the cut would have flooded with blood, not red but pink because her skin was wet, washing in a pale, wide stream down her ankle bone and foot, the way she would have cursed and pressed the cut with her fingers. Angie reached out and touched the scar. In the moment before Mrs. Salter jerked her leg away, Angie could feel a tiny seam beneath the tip of her finger, as though someone had taken two neat stitches there with white thread. Inside the scar was Mrs. Salter's soul. The soul was just that small, tiny and white as a star. For one moment she understood the realness of Mrs.

Salter to herself, how to Mrs. Salter the world radiated out from her own body, and Angie could feel that for every person in the room at once, she felt the room's hundred centers.

Mrs. Salter jerked her leg away.

The noise of the room had flooded back in. One of the noises was someone laughing, yelping wildly. Someone had said, "Is that girl okay?" Someone, Jess, had said, "Stop it, Angie, stop it, *stop* it." And then Jess had run out of the room and that had seemed even funnier.

Sam put his hand on her arm. "Angie? We're supposed to be going out to the truck."

Angie was bent over, arms around herself, face against her thighs. Nothing, she was thinking. Nothing, nothing could make her fall apart in front of Jess again. She would be okay as long as she was careful, as long as she kept her hands out of sight, as long as she kept her thoughts on track. As long as she focused on the small details, as long as she made that be enough, as long as she made that be everything.

They rode the half-mile to the barns in the back of a rattling Ford pick-up. On sharp turns the key sometimes fell out of the ignition. The wind had died down to an occasional blast, sharp enough to pierce through Angie's coat. Though the sun was weak, the snow on the ground shone. They jolted slowly down the road, past the Residences—Yellow House, White House, Ivy House—past the Director's House, past the orchard that held beehives in the summer. Sheep lifted masked, unsurprised faces to watch them. The llama had matted hair and a narrow, haughty countenance. As the truck passed, he detached from the flock and jogged mincingly toward the fence.

At the cowshed, the college student turned off the ignition; the truck continued to shake for a minute longer. Angie climbed up onto the rusty ledge of the truck-bed, jumped heavily down. Pulling her scarf over her nose and mouth—as she breathed she tasted ice crystals and damp wool—she went around to the passenger-side door. Her hands were clumsy in her leather gloves, and it took three tries to unhook the baling wire that held the door. When the wire finally slipped free, she took a few awkward steps backward in the high snow, holding the door open. Sam Manning had been riding in the cab. He clambered down, and then together he and Angie wired the door shut again.

Coming in from the snow, the inside of the barn seemed dim. Written above each stall were the names of the cow's sire, her dam, the bull she'd been mated with, and then the cow's own name: Molly, Maggie, Jenny. Angie helped to unclip the cows from their long chains and herd them out into the frozen side yard. Jenny went uncomplainingly, but when Angie went back for Maggie, she balked at the doorway. Angie hit her, then set her shoulder against the cow's heavy haunch and pushed. Maggie set her hooves, tensing back. Her huge eye rolled wildly. Beneath Angie's cheek, the cow's coarse hair smelled of rumen, straw, manure, at once pleasing and abrasive. "Come *on*," Angie said, banging the cow with her shoulder. Maggie didn't budge, and then all at once she gave in and came unstuck. As though it were what she'd intended all along, she trotted out. In the yard, the cows crowded together, standing head-to-rump, their breath rising in dense white clouds. Angie unzipped her jacket and stood, hands on hips. Clouds of her breath—smaller than the cows' and more transparent—rose in the icy air.

Back inside, she pitchforked up yesterday's matted straw. Mixed in were crumpled paper towels, stained purple with teat disinfectant the milkers used. The barn was warm and close; Angie took off her jacket, hanging it on a nail. Betsy turned on the radio, an ancient black Realistic balanced between two exposed wall studs, dialing until she found a faint heavy metal song, fuzzed with static.

"No voices," said Sam Manning.

"No voices," the team leader agreed. Betsy rolled her eyes, tried to find another station. Finally she turned off the radio.

"They're all going to talk *some*time," she said. "There's going to be *commercials*."

In silence, they used brooms to sweep the floor clear of the last chaff. Then Sam Manning hosed down the concrete. Sam was more than twice Angie's age, someone who outside the farm she would never have even known. In this odd, new life, though, he was her friend, her only real one, the only person who laughed when she made a joke instead of looking worried. They'd first found each other on Movie Night because they both voted for videos that lost. They wanted *Chinatown* instead of *Pretty Woman*, *Do the Right Thing* instead of *Ghost*, anything instead of *Sister Act*. Angie went to the Movie Nights anyway—she had nothing better to do. She and Sam sat in back and made fun of the dialogue. *It must be hard to give up something so valuable*, the concierge said to Richard Gere, who blinked stoically.

When Sam was twenty, voices had told him to kill his twin sister, then himself. He'd gone to her college dorm and stabbed her in the stomach. She screamed and rolled away and his second thrust went wild, tearing open her arm. He managed to stab her a third time, in the thigh, before breaking down in tears. Sundays, Sam's sister came to the farm, and they sat together smoking. She was also burly, also iron-haired. Her limp was barely noticeable, but if she pushed up her sleeve, a knotty scar ran from her right elbow down her forearm, almost to the wrist. There had been such extensive nerve damage that she couldn't use her right hand. It stunned Angie what could be lived around in a family:

surely it shouldn't be possible, their sitting together on the stone wall by the sheep barn. She'd seen the sister reach for Sam's lighter, dipping her left hand into his shirt pocket as naturally as if it were her own.

At nine-thirty, they took a break. Hannah drove down from the kitchen, swinging herself out of the truck cab. Her jeans were made up more of patches than the original denim. She reached back into the truck for chocolate chip cookies and a thermos of cider.

The cookies were hot from the oven. The Residents and Staff stood in the lee of the barn, eating the cookies and smoking, ashing into a coffee can of sand. Angie, who didn't smoke, wandered over to the fence and watched the cows. It had gotten warmer; she balled up her scarf and stuffed it in her pocket.

Hannah came up beside her. "Why do you think everyone here smokes?"

"Everyone did at the hospital, too. I don't know why." Angie wiped the corners of her mouth to make sure she didn't have chocolate smeared there.

"It drives me—" Hannah cut herself off. "It's annoying."

Angie said shyly, "I like your jeans."

"Yeah?" Hannah looked down, considering them.

Angie's sweater snagged on the fence. She pulled it free, leaving a wisp of green wool in the rough wood. She rubbed her mouth again, in case there really was chocolate there. Suggesting to herself things she might say to Hannah, and then rejecting them, she pretended to be wholly absorbed in watching the cows. They looked miserable in the field, barely grazing.

Hannah said, "I was hoping maybe we could talk sometime."

"Yeah? I mean, sure."

"Before lunch? We could take a walk. Or this afternoon I'm driving Town Trip."

Angie shook her head. "This afternoon I'm meeting my friend from high school."

"Time," the team leader called.

Hannah asked, "She's visiting?"

"I'm meeting her on Town Trip."

"Why doesn't she come to the farm?"

"I don't know. She can't come for very long." Actually, Angie had told Jess that only family could visit the farm.

"Angie!" The team leader pulled on his stocking cap and said to Hannah, "You're holding up my best worker."

Angie felt herself grinning with stupid happiness. She said, "I could talk after this. Before lunch."

They walked through the soft snow on one of the old logging trails behind the farm. Hannah asked her about getting sick and the hospital, which Angie had only talked about with doctors and other patients. Telling someone her own age, someone who hadn't lived in the System, made her queasy. Still, she'd told the story so many times that the words came easily.

The day had turned beautiful, warm for the first time in months. When Angie said she'd been misdiagnosed in the hospital, Hannah stopped short. "They misdiagnosed you?"

"They thought I was schizophrenic."

"So they had you on—?"

"Mellaril? It's an antipsychotic?" Blushing, she told Hannah how Mellaril had made her neck and jaw muscles stiffen so tight that she couldn't talk. She told how sometimes she'd fallen out so badly she'd been put into Isolation, where she threw herself against the wall until aides arrived to sedate her.

"I can't imagine you doing that."

A fist in Angie's chest, tight for months, unclenched a little. "I can't either, really." She looked at Hannah for the first time and saw on her face neither pity nor revulsion.

Talking faster, she said they'd given her tranquilizers to counteract the Mellaril, how on tranquilizers the world stretched out thick and flat. Her words started tripping over each other, like when she was manic, and she said, "Slow down, slow down. I know I need to slow down." She hit the side of her head with her fist and grinned.

She told Hannah that parts of her past seemed to belong to other people, to a girl watching television without comprehension on the ward. Or, before that, a crazy girl who broke windows, who had torn her books apart, who had slept with people she barely knew. Hannah said *Jesus* and *Wow* and, twice, *It's the world that's crazy.*

Melting ice dripped from the undersides of branches. If Angie closed her eyes, she could hear the drops all around her, running together into a sound like tap water. She probably looked crazy, walking with her eyes closed. She opened them and said, "It's almost spring."

"People say spring's a hard time at the farm. A lot of people have breaks."

Angie glanced at her, but Hannah didn't seem to be remembering Angie as one of the group at risk for breaks. Trying to use the same casual tone, Angie asked, "I wonder why in the spring? I'd think, like, a month ago, when it was so gray all the time. And, you know, cold."

"Apparently the change does it. In winter people hold together as long as it seems things are going to get better. Then when things do start getting better—I can't explain it well. We had a training on it. They said until things stabilize again mid-summer, April's the last good month."

They'd reached the end of the trail. Hannah turned to hug her and said, "Thank you for telling me so much. You're a very strong person."

Angie hugged her back tightly, and afterward, all through lunch, she talked to Hannah in her head. She clarified some of the things she'd said earlier. Sitting in the TV room, waiting for the Town Trip, she told Hannah silently about her younger brother, the way that he sulked and snapped on visits. She said, *You've seen him right?* and in her head Hannah said, *I think maybe. Reddish hair?* She confided to Hannah that she hadn't taken her meds this morning; she hoped it would make her shake less. She was going to take a double dose tonight, as soon as Jess left.

Jess.

She was too wired to sit here. She had half an hour before the van left for Town Trip. Out on the front porch, she pulled her jacket tighter around her body and started walking. Wind stirred up small eddies from the surface of the snow. She turned and cut up into the woods.

In the woods, the snow was deeper. Dark tree branches rubbed together, moaning. The high snow made walking hard; she stopped to unzip her jacket. She thought about lying down to make a snow angel, then—as she started to lower herself—thought maybe there was something crazy about lying down in the snow and straightened and went on.

Hannah lived in one of the small Staff cabins out here in the woods, little houses without plumbing. When Angie had been on the Grounds Team she'd helped deliver wood to these cottages. She'd still been on the wrong meds then—Haldol, a little better than Mellaril. Her few memories of the insides of the cabins had a dreamy, unanchored quality: a red blanket, a shelf of books, a propped-up postcard of a painting.

The clearing between Angie and Hannah's cabin was wide and very still. Thin smoke twisted from the chimney. She saw a small brown hawk the moment before it launched itself from the tree into the air. There was the soft thump of snow falling onto snow, the *hush, hush* of wings. Walking through snow had soaked Angie's pants to the knees and she shivered.

Just as she was turning to go, the cabin door opened.

Hannah emerged, walked a few feet, drew down her jeans and crouched. In the woods, everything looked like a pen and ink drawing: white snow, gray smoke, black trees and the cold blue wash of shadows at their bases. And Hannah seemed drawn with ink, too, as she stood again, pulling up her jeans. Short dark hair, the white undershirt she wore, then the closing of the cabin door behind her.

The wind paused. Angie walked toward the cabin. From inside came the chirrup of the woodstove door. A log was thrown on the fire, and then silence stretched over the clearing. Where Hannah had been, the snow was pocked yellow. Angie felt oddly exhilarated. She crouched, using her teeth to pull off her mitten and put her hand above the surface, feeling warmth mixed with the cold air rising against her palm.

The Town Trip was to Sheepskill, thirty miles from the farm. Hannah parked the old van behind the health food store. Hitting the parking lot, the Residents were like a clump of fish being released into a tank, turning disoriented in place for a moment, then separating. Two of the lowest-functioners headed together toward Sheepskill's supermarket. Others walked in the direction of the drugstore, the record store.

Angie lingered near the van. Kicking snow from her boot sole, she said, "Today's the day I'm meeting Jess. Who I told you about."

"I remember." Hannah finished writing the names of Residents who had come to town, then tossed the checklist onto the front seat. "Are you nervous?"

Angie's stomach kept twisting, like a rag being wrung out. "No. I guess a little. I haven't seen her since before the hospital."

"It'll be fine," Hannah said, pulling the van door shut. She reached and touched Angie's arm briefly. Then she took two steps backward, waved. "Go on. It will be fun."

As a meeting place Angie had chosen The Daily Grind, Sheepskill's less popular coffee shop, where they weren't as likely to run into other Residents. Walking down Main Street, she tried to see the town as Jess might. The stores had high, square fronts and faux-nineteenth-century signs, or else real 1950's ones. The banked snow was melting, filling the street with gray slush. In front of the gas station was a boy her age with a smudgy mustache, jaw raw with acne. He lifted a mop from a bucket of hot water, rolling the handle between his ungloved hands so the strings flared into a circle, then bent to swab the sidewalk. His body, beneath the blue-gray jacket, was beautiful. In the cold air, clouds of steam rose from the bucket. A handmade sign advertised free maps with a full tank of gas.

The Daily Grind was at the top of a steep hill. The slush made walking difficult: with every step, Angie slid half a step back, arms out to her sides for balance. Even though she did physical work, she'd gained weight on lithium, and she reached the top of the hill breathing heavily. While she tried to pull her clothes straight on the café's porch, a woman came out, holding the hand of a little boy. He had hockey player hair, cut very short on top and left long in back. The boy said, "Mom, I want—"

The mother yanked his arm, hard. hissing, "I told you don't say *I want*."

Jess stood as Angie came in. Angie's fear that she wouldn't recognize Jess had been crazy: she looked so familiar that Angie didn't think *There she is*, but *Oh*.

*There* you are.

Jess hated her height; she slouched, shoulders rounded forward. Her long hair was pulled back in a ponytail. As she stepped forward, Angie stepped back, then realized Jess had meant to hug her. They bumped together awkwardly, Angie's hands still in her pockets.

"You look great!" Jess said.

"The coffee's pretty good here."

"It's been so long since I've seen you!"

"Do you want some coffee? I'll get it."

"No, I'll get it." Jess reached back for her purse. "My treat."

Once, Angie would have said—what? Something sarcastic about Jess's generosity. She sat, then looked quickly around the café, relaxing when she saw she'd been right: no other Residents. Inside her pockets, Angie's hands were trembling, despite skipping her Eskalith. She needed to calm down or she'd sound like a mental patient: the response to *you look great* was not *the coffee here's pretty good*.

"Here," Jess said. "I got you a muffin too."

If she gripped the cup hard enough, it stilled her hands. The coffee was black, bitter and delicious. The farm didn't have coffee. On town trips, Residents bought jars of instant and brought them back. At the farm, tablespoons of dried coffee were a currency as valuable as cigarettes, more valuable than real money.

There hadn't been coffee in the hospital either. The first morning last fall that she'd woken up on the locked ward, she had such a bad caffeine headache she'd shivered and vomited. She'd told the nurses she was dying, she had a brain tumor, she was descended from Scottish kings and she was dying on a shitty filthy ward. She took off her clothes and lay down on the floor of the bathroom. The small, cold tiles under her cheek had, for a moment, brought her shockingly back to herself ("Angie," she'd said, "Angie. Angie. Angie. Angie."), but then the Nursing Aides tried to move her and she'd become terrified, scratching and biting, and that was the first time she'd ended up in Isolation.

Jess said, "Your brother probably tells you everything about school."

Angie shook her head. "Luke doesn't tell me anything. We've never been exactly close."

Jess visibly relaxed. She began talking about who had broken up, who had gotten into what college, the swim team. In the café were two geeky junior-high boys playing chess, a woman with a sleeping baby, a middle-aged man sketching. No one had any reason to think Angie was anything other than what she appeared, a girl in jeans, drinking coffee with a friend on a Saturday. She tried to listen to Jess, but her attention was on the street outside the door, willing Residents to stay away. So she wouldn't turn to look, she held herself stiff. Each time the door opened, she felt herself jerk in her seat. Jess smiled at something she was saying and Angie told herself, *smile*. She was relieved to realize Jess, in her narration of the last three months, wasn't going to mention why Angie hadn't been at school. Jess said some of the cheerleaders had been booted off the squad for coming to a game drunk. She laughed. Late, Angie laughed too.

Jess looked down at her cup. She picked it up and swirled it.

Outside, a car moved carefully up the street, headlights on. In the slushy snow, its tires made a sound like ripping silk. It was three-thirty in the afternoon, the light beginning to fade. Jess at last looked up. They smiled at each other helplessly. "More coffee?" Jess asked.

If she drank more coffee she would be sick. She could just hold the cup and not drink. "Sure. I'll get it."

"Sit down, sit down."

She sat down. Her hands were too trembly, anyway, to carry two mugs without spilling.

Jess bustled over to the counter, joked with the girl working. It was Angie, not Jess, who was usually good with strangers, but suddenly Jess had taken on the role of The Competent Friend. On the way back to the table, she raised one hand—holding a full cup of coffee!—and used the back of her thumb to push hair out of her eyes. She sat down, saying, "I'm so tired." She bent her head, resting it on her arms.

While her head was lowered, Angie said quickly, "The farm's like—My parents think I have to be there. The doctor doesn't even think I have what the first doctor thought I have. No one has a clue, really." It seemed true as she said it.

Jess sat up. "You must be so pissed."

"It's not so bad. People are pretty normal."

"In your letter you said they were pretty crazy."

What had she written Jess? "Well, some people. Not most people, though. I'm friends with this girl, Hannah, she's just taking a semester off from school."

"So it's like that? I mean, some people are.... Some people need to be there but other people are just..."

"Just there." For the first time all afternoon, her footing began to feel sure, not just because she'd found a softened, not totally untrue, way to describe the farm, but also because next to Hannah, Jess would seem awkward and unremarkable. "I mean, I wasn't going to come back to school in the middle of the semester. I think what I had before was a nervous breakdown, trying to do too many things at once. Everyone freaked out, but that was pretty much all it was."

"You know, that's what I thought. I mean, it's not like you're psycho."

"The hospital will make you psycho, though." You weren't allowed to use words like psycho or crazy at the farm; saying them felt like throwing off heavy blankets. "I was just talking to Hannah about how when I was in there, at the hospital, everyone was treating me like I was really sick, my parents were all—" she made her face pinched and solemn. "And everyone was saying I'd have to take meds, medication, forever. You begin believing it."

"In the hospital, I should've come see you."

"No, you shouldn't have."

Angie felt the conversation set its hooves and stall. She said something she'd said successfully to Hannah: "When I think of the hospital, I don't know who I am."

"What's that supposed to mean, you don't know who you are?"

"I mean it's confusing. I think about things I . . . Jesus. I mean, it's the world that's fucked up."

Jess pushed some crumbs into a line.

"I mean, isn't it?"

"I don't know. I guess so. I don't know."

The door opened and shut. This time, they both turned. Sam Manning, stomping ice from his boots, raised his hand in greeting.

"Who's that?"

"A Res—Someone from the farm." At least Sam was normal. Wasn't he? She had the time he was in line to think what to say about him to Jess, but her brain felt slow. She raised her coffee and found she'd drunk it all.

Near them, a little girl was kneeling on the floor. Two women talked at the table above. Periodically, one of them called down, "Are you okay, Liza?"

The girl didn't respond. She had straight bangs that fell into her eyes and a wind-up toy, an alien with arms hugged to its body and three eyes across its forehead. The little girl wound a key in its side and it ran awkwardly, body pitched forward so that with each step it teetered, seemed barely to catch itself from falling.

Angie said, "They always make aliens look just like humans with one thing different."

"What?"

Angie's hands were jumping on the mug. She put them between her knees, pressing to still them. "Do you mean what did I say or what did I mean?"

"Which thing is different?"

"I don't mean there's a specific thing, I mean they change something."

"What are you talking about?" Jess looked suddenly on the verge of tears. "You're not even acting like you're happy to see me. I don't know what's wrong with you."

"Nothing's wrong with me!"

Jess flinched and looked away.

Sam was making his way over. He had a shambling walk—was that weird?—and blue down vest (weird?) and carried his mug carefully, watching to make sure it didn't spill. "Hey, Angie."

"Hey."

There was a silence, then Jess introduced herself. "I know," said Sam. "I've heard a lot about you."

"You have." Jess raised an eyebrow at Angie, who looked away. Jess asked Sam, "Do you want to sit down?"

"I guess, for a minute." Sitting, he looked around the café, cracking his knuckles. On his right hand, the fingers were stained dark yellow with nicotine. "How long was your drive?"

"Four hours," Jess said. "The roads were pretty good."

"You were lucky. Last night we had a windstorm."

"In New Hampshire, we had a windstorm last year that killed two people. A tree came down on their car."

Angie relaxed a little. This was a normal conversation. She was pretty sure. Sam asked about the colleges Jess had applied to, and Jess listed the places she'd gotten in and the places she hadn't. She thought she'd go to Bates. Had he gone to college? He had. Tufts University. "But I didn't—"

Angie blurted, "What do you think Hannah does on these trips?"

"Hannah?" Sam turned toward her. He was so big and so slow-moving. He said, "I saw her at the record store. I'm actually supposed to talk to her later. She said she already talked to you."

"Talked to me?"

"For her paper."

"Her paper."

"Her psych paper. She said you guys did an interview this morning." He looked at her, then frowned. "Are you okay?"

"No. No. I just—right." An interview. She lifted her mug—no, all gone, she put it down. Too hard: it skipped and started to totter and Jess grabbed to steady it. Jess and Sam had identical expressions on their faces. They looked like her parents had begun looking at her last fall, wary and assessing. She laughed loudly. "You don't have to look like that."

"Like what?" Sam asked.

"Like I've just run over your dog."

"I don't have a dog."

Angie laughed again. She rolled her eyes at Jess, then saw that Sam was watching her. She froze, halfway through the motion, mouth still open, eyes wide.

"Okay," he said. He pushed back from the table and smiled weakly. "I guess you girls need time alone. I forgot how long it's been since you saw each other."

Jess said, "Stay, it's okay, we've had forever to talk."

Sam shook his head. Angie remembered how he'd said his sister was his only real friend. She hated the emptiness of his life. When he stood and said, "Well . . ." she let him walk away.

At four, ten minutes before the van would leave, Angie and Jess stood outside the café saying good-bye. The light had become grainy; in a half-hour it would be dark. Low above the latched black branches of trees, the moon was barely visible against the equally pale sky. A parked car, finned and low, its headlights left on, floated at the curb like a blind fish.

"I have to go," Angie said.

Suddenly, too late, she felt how much she'd missed Jess. They used to say good-bye like this, lingering at a corner. They'd call each other sometimes ten times a night. For a moment, it seemed homesickness would knock her down.

"Well, bye," Jess said.

"You have a long drive."

Jess shrugged. She bounced her keys in her gloved hand, looking off. Then she looked at Angie. "You're okay, right? Are you okay?"

How many times removed was she from okay? She nodded, tightening her coat.

As she started down the hill from Jess, she could see—spread out through Sheepskill—other Residents, straggling back singly and in pairs. She saw the whole town as a pattern of streets, glazed with late-afternoon light, leading to the van. When she turned, Jess was still standing in front of the café, watching her. Angie gave a hearty, whole-arm wave, the kind people on boats gave to people on shore.

At the van, a few people milled around, taking advantage of the last few minutes off-farm. She put her hand into her pocket and found, still unopened, the envelope holding her meds.

Pretending to cough, she bent and dropped the crumpled packet in the snow, quickly burying it with her foot. As she straightened, her face burned, but no one seemed to have seen. Ahead of her in line, Doug chanted, "Thing of beauty, thing of beauty." Someone else—low, so Hannah wouldn't hear—said, "Shut up, Doug," and he did.

Angie walked hunched over through the van to a seat in the back. Two Residents talked loudly. Hannah asked, "Julie, is your seatbelt on?"

"Yup."

"Angie? Seatbelt?"

Out the window, the air was lined, as though with sleet: the last few moments between dusk and true evening.

"She's got it on," someone said.

Hannah backed and feinted, backed and feinted, turning the van around. They drove slowly out of the lot. Angie leaned her head against the cold, rattling window glass. The passivity of being in a van made her feel like a small child, as though it were years ago and she were riding the school bus. In second grade, Jess had had a brown rabbit coat, so soft that Angie had found excuses—the bus going over a bump—for her hand to brush Jess's sleeve. They'd been best friends, by then, four months. During math time, they drew insulting pictures of each other naked. "This is you," Jess whispered, drawing salami-shaped breasts on a straight-sided woman. "Well, this is *you*," Angie whispered, and scrawled armpit hair onto her own picture, pressing so hard the pencil lines shone silver.

The van turned a corner and Angie saw the real Jess, head down, walking to her car. Angie started to duck, but Jess wasn't looking her way. She had her parka hood up and her arms around herself for warmth. As Angie watched, she broke suddenly into a run. Still hugging herself, she ran awkwardly, body pitched forward so that with each step she teetered, seeming barely to catch herself from falling.

# The Kind of Light That Shines on Texas

REGINALD MCKNIGHT

I never liked Marvin Pruitt. Never liked him, never knew him, even though there were only three of us in the class. Three black kids. In our school there were fourteen class-rooms of thirty-odd white kids (in '66, they considered Chicanos provisionally white) and three or four black kids. Primary school in primary colors. Neat division. Alphabetized. They didn't stick us in the back, or arrange us by degrees of hue, apartheidlike. This was real integration, a ten-to-one ratio as tidy as upperclass landscaping. If it all worked, you could have ten white kids all to yourself. They could talk to you, get the feel of you, scrutinize you bone deep if they wanted to. They seldom wanted to, and that was fine with me for two reasons. The first was that their scrutiny was irritating. How do you comb your hair—why do you comb your hair—may I please touch your hair—were the kinds of questions they asked. This is no way to feel at home. The second reason was Marvin. He embar-rassed me. He smelled bad, was at least two grades behind, was hostile, dark-skinned, homely, close-mouthed. I feared him for his size, pitied him for his dress, watched him all the time. Marveled at him, mystified, astonished, uneasy.

He had the habit of spitting on his right arm, juicing it down till it would glisten. He would start in immediately after taking his seat when we'd finished with the Pledge of Allegiance, "The Yellow Rose of Texas," "The Eyes of Texas

Are upon You," and "Mistress Shady." Marvin would rub his spit-flecked arm with his left hand, rub and roll as if polishing an ebony pool cue. Then he would rest his head in the crook of his arm, sniffing, huffing deep like black-jacket boys huff bagsful of acrylics. After ten minutes or so, his eyes would close, heavy. He would sleep until recess. Mrs. Wickham would let him.

There was one other black kid in our class. A girl they named Ah-so. I never learned what she did to earn this name. There was nothing Asian about this big-shouldered girl. She was the tallest, heaviest kid in school. She was quiet, but I don't think any one of us was subtle or sophisticated enough to nickname our classmates according to any but physical attributes. Fat kids were called Porky or Butterball, skinny ones were called Stick or Ichabod. Ah-so was big, thick, and African. She would impassively sit, sullen, silent as Marvin. She wore the same dark blue pleated skirt every day, the same ruffled white blouse every day. Her skin always shone as if worked by Marvin's palms and fingers. I never spoke one word to her, nor she to me.

Of the three of us, Mrs. Wickham called only on Ah-so and me. Ah-so never answered one question, correctly or incorrectly, so far as I can recall. She wasn't stupid. When asked to read aloud she read well, seldom stumbling over long words, reading with humor and expression. But when Wickham asked her about Farmer Brown and how many cows, or the capital of Vermont, or the date of this war or that, Ah-so never spoke. Not one word. But you always felt she could have answered those questions if she'd wanted to. I sensed tension, embarrassment, or anger in Ah-so's reticence. She simply refused to speak. There was something unshakable about her, some core so impenetrably solid, you got the feeling that it you stood too close to her she could eat your thoughts like a black star eats light. I didn't despise Ah-so as I despised Marvin. There was nothing malevolent about her. She sat like a great icon in the back of the classroom, tranquil, guarded, sealed up, watchful. She was close to sixteen, and it was my guess she'd given up on school. Perhaps she was just obliging the wishes of her family, sticking it out till the law could no longer reach her.

There were at least half a dozen older kids in our class. Besides Marvin and Ah-so, there was Oakley, who sat behind me, whispering threats into my ear; Varna Willard with the large breasts; Eddie Limon, who played bass for a high school rock band; and Lawrence Ridderbeck, who everyone said had a kid and a wife. You couldn't expect me to know anything about Texan educational practices of the 1960s, so I never knew why there were so many older kids in my sixth-grade class. After all, I was just a boy and had transferred into the school around midyear. My father, an air force sergeant, had been sent to Viet Nam. The air force sent my mother, my sister, Claire, and me to Connolly Air Force Base, which during the war housed "unaccompanied wives." I'd been to so many schools in my short life that I ceased wondering about their differences. All I knew about the Texas schools was that they weren't afraid to flunk you.

Yet though I was only twelve then, I had a good idea why Wickham never once called on Marvin, why she let him snooze in the crook of his polished arm. I knew why she would press her lips together, and narrow her eyes at me whenever I correctly answered a question, rare as that was. I know why she badgered Ah-so with questions everyone knew Ah-so would never even consider answering. Wickham didn't like us. She wasn't gross about it, but it was clear she didn't want us around. She would prove her dislike day after day with little stories and jokes. "I just want to share with you all," she would say, "a little riddle my daughter told me at the supper table the other day.

Now, where do you go when you injure your knee?" Then one, two, or all three of her pets would say for the rest of us, "We don't know, Miz Wickham," in that skin-chilling way suck-asses speak, "Where?" "Why, to Africa," Wickham would say, "where the knee grows."

The thirty-odd white kids would laugh, and I would look across the room at Marvin. He'd be asleep. I would glance back at Ah-so. She'd be sitting still as a projected image, staring down at her desk. I, myself, would smile at Wickham's stupid jokes, sometimes fake a laugh. I tried to show her that at least one of us was alive and alert, even though her jokes hurt. I sucked ass, too, I suppose. But I wanted her to understand more that anything that I was not like her other nigra children, that I was worthy of more than the non-attention and the negative attention she paid Marvin and Ah-so. I hated her, but never showed it. No one could safely contradict that woman. She knew all kinds of tricks to demean, control, and punish you. And she could swing her two-foot paddle as fluidly as a big-league slugger swings a bat. You didn't speak in Wickham's class unless she spoke to you first. You didn't chew gum, or wear "hood" hair. You didn't drag your feet, curse, pass notes, hold hands with the opposite sex. Most especially, you didn't say anything bad about the Aggies, Governor Connolly, LBJ, Sam Houston, or Waco. You did the forbidden and she would get you. It was that simple.

She never got me, though. Never gave her reason to. But she could have invented reasons. She did a lot of that. I can't be sure, but I used to think she pitied me because my father was in Viet Nam and my uncle A. J. had recently died there. Whenever she would tell one of her racist jokes, she would always glance at me, preface the joke with, "Now don't you nigra children take offense. This is all in fun, you know. I just want to share with you all something Coach Gilchrest told me th'other day." She would tell her joke, and glance at me again. I'd giggle, feeling a little queasy. "I'm half Irish," she would chuckle, "and you should hear some of those Irish jokes." She never told any, and I never really expected her to. I just did my Tom-thing. I kept my shoes shined, my desk neat, answered her questions as best I could, never brought gum to school, never cursed, never slept in class. I wanted to show her we were not all the same.

I tried to show them all, all thirty-odd, that I was different. It worked to some degree, but not very well. When some article was stolen from someone's locker or desk, Marvin, not I, was the first accused. I'd be second. Neither Marvin nor Ah-so nor I were ever chosen for certain classroom honors—"Pledge leader," "flag holder," "noise monitor," "paper passer-outer," but Mrs. Wickham once let me be "eraser duster." I was proud. I didn't even care about the cracks my fellow students made about my finally having turned the right color. I had done something that Marvin, in the deeps of his never-ending sleep, couldn't even dream of doing. Jack Preston, a kid who sat in front of me, asked me one day at recess whether I was embarrassed about Marvin. "Can you believe that guy?" I said. "He's like a pig or something. Makes me sick."

"Does it make you ashamed to be colored?"

"No," I said, but I meant yes. Yes, if you insist on thinking us all the same. Yes, if his faults are mine, his weaknesses inherent in me.

"I'd be," said Jack.

I made no reply. I was ashamed. Ashamed for not defending Marvin and ashamed that Marvin even existed. But if it had occurred to me, I would have asked Jack whether he was ashamed of being white because of Oakley. Oakley, "Oak Tree," Kelvin "Oak Tree" Oakley. He was sixteen and proud of it. He made it clear to everyone, including Wickham, that his life's ambition was to stay in school one more year, till he'd be old enough to enlist in the army. "Them slopes got my brother," he would say, "I'mna sign up and git me a few slopes. Gonna kill them bastards dead-er'n shit." Oakley, so far as anyone knew, was and always had been the oldest kid in his family. But no one contradicted him. He would, as anyone would tell you, "snap yer neck jest as soon as look at you." Not a boy in class, excepting Marvin and myself, had been able to avoid Oakley's pink bellies, Texas titty twisters, moon pie punches, or worse. He didn't bother Marvin, I suppose, because Marvin was closer to his size and age, and because Marvin spent five sixths of the school day asleep. Marvin probably never crossed Oakley's mind. And to say that Oakley hadn't bothered me is not to say he had no intention of ever doing so. In fact, this haphazard sketch of hairy fingers, slash of eyebrow, explosion of acne, elbows, and crooked teeth, swore almost daily that he'd like to kill me.

Naturally, I feared him. Though we were about the same height, he outweighed me by no less than forty pounds. He talked, stood, smoked, and swore like a man. No one, except for Mrs. Wickham, the principal, and the coach, ever laid a finger on him. And even Wickham knew that the hot lines she laid on him merely amused him. He would smile out at the classroom, goofy and bashful, as she laid down the two, five, or maximum ten strokes on him. Often he would wink, or surreptitiously flash us the thumb as Wickham worked on him. When she was finished, Oakley would walk so cool back to his seat you'd think he was on wheels. He'd slide into his chair, sniff the air, and say, "Somethin's burnin. Do y'all smell smoke? I swanee, I smell smoke and fahr back here." If he had made these cracks and never threatened me, I might have grown to admire Oakley, even liked him a little. But he hated me, and took every opportunity during the six-hour school day to make me aware of this. "Some Sambo's gittin his ass broke open one of these days," he'd mumble. "I wanna fight somebody. Need to keep in shape till I git to Nam."

I never said anything to him for the longest time. I pretended not to hear him, pretended not to notice his sour breath on my neck and ear. "Yep," he'd whisper. "Coonies keep y' in good shape for slope killin." Day in, day out, that's the kind of thing I'd pretend not to hear. But one day when the rain dropped down like lead balls, and the cold air made your skin looked plucked, Oakley whispered to me, "My brother tells me it rains like this in Nam. Maybe I oughta go out at recess and break your ass open today. Nice and cool so you don't sweat. Nice and wet to clean up the blood." I said nothing for at least half a minute, then I turned half right and said, "Thought you said your brother was dead." Oakley, silent himself, for a time, poked me in the back with his pencil and hissed, "*Yer* dead." Wickham cut her eyes our way, and it was over.

It was hardest avoiding him in gym class. Especially when we played murderball. Oakley always aimed his throws at me. He threw with unblinking intensity, his teeth gritting, his neck veining, his face flushing, his black hair sweeping over one eye. He could throw hard, but the balls were squishy and harmless. In fact, I found his misses more intimidating than his hits. The balls would whizz by, thunder against the folded bleachers. They rattled as though a locomotive were passing through them. I would duck, dodge, leap as if he were throwing grenades. But he always hit me, sooner or later. And after a while I noticed that the other boys would avoid throwing at me, as if I belonged to Oakley.

One day, however, I was surprised to see that Oakley was throwing at everyone else but me. He was uncommonly accurate, too; kids were falling like tin cans. Since no one was throwing at me, I spent most of the game watching Oakley cut this one and that one down. Finally, he and I were the only ones left on the court. Try as he would, he couldn't hit me, nor I him. Coach Gilchrest blew his whistle and told Oakley and me to bring the red rubber balls to the equipment locker. I was relieved I'd escaped Oakley's stinging throws for once. I was feeling triumphant, full of myself. As Oakley and I approached Gilchrest, I thought about saying something friendly to Oakley: Good game, Oak Tree, I would say. Before I could speak, though, Gilchrest said, "All right boys, there's five minutes left in the period. Y'all are so good, looks like, you're gonna have to play like men. No boundaries, no catch outs, and you gotta hit your opponent three times in order to win. Got me?"

We nodded.

"And you're gonna use these," said Gilchrest, pointing to three volleyballs at his feet. "And you better believe they're pumped full. Oates, you start at that end of the court. Oak Tree, you're at th'other end. Just like usual, I'll set the balls at mid-court, and when I blow my whistle I want y'all to haul your cheeks to the middle and th'ow for all you're worth. Got me?" Gilchrest nodded at our nods, then added, "Remember, no boundaries, right?"

I at my end, Oakley at his, Gilchrest blew his whistle. I was faster than Oakley and scooped up a ball before he'd covered three quarters of his side. I aimed, threw, and popped him right on the knee. "One-zip!" I heard Gilchrest shout. The ball bounced off his knee and shot right back into my hands. I hurried my throw and missed. Oakley bent down, clutched the two remaining balls. I remember being amazed that he could palm each ball, run full out, and throw left-handed or right-handed without a shade of awkwardness. I spun, ran, but one of Oakley's throws glanced off the back of my head. "One-one!" hollered Gilchrest. I fell and spun on my ass as the other ball came sailing at me. I caught it. "He's out!" I yelled. Gilchrest's voice boomed, "No catch outs. Three hits. Three hits." I leapt to my feet as Oakley scrambled across the floor for another ball. I chased him down, leapt, and heaved the ball hard as he drew himself erect. The ball hit him dead in the face, and he went down flat. He rolled around, cupping his hands over his nose. Gilchrest sped to his side, helped him to his feet, asked him whether he was okay. Blood flowed from Oakley's nose, dripped in startlingly bright spots on the floor, his shoes, Gilchrest's shirt. The coach removed Oakley's t-shirt and pressed it against the big kid's nose to stanch the bleeding. As they walked past me toward the office I mumbled an apology to Oakley, but couldn't catch his reply. "You watch your filthy mouth, boy," said Gilchrest to Oakley.

The locker room was unnaturally quiet as I stepped into its steamy atmosphere. Eyes clicked in my direction, looked away. After I was out of my shorts, had my towel wrapped around me, my shower kit in hand, Jack Preston and Brian Nailor approached me. Preston's hair was combed slick and plastic-looking. Nailor's stood up like frozen flames. Nailor smiled at me with his big teeth and pale eyes. He poked my arm with a finger. "You fucked up," he said.

"I tried to apologize."

"Won't do you no good," said Preston.

"I swanee," said Nailor.

"It's part of the game," I said. "It was an accident. Wasn't my idea to use volleyballs."

"Don't matter," Preston said. "He's jest lookin for an excuse to fight you."

"I never done nothing to him."

"Don't matter," said Nailor. "He don't like you."

"Brian's right, Clint. He'd jest as soon kill you as look at you."

"I never done nothing to him."

"Look," said Preston, "I know him pretty good. And jest between you and me, it's 'cause you're a city boy—"

"Whadda you mean? I've never—"

"He don't like your clothes—"

"And he don't like the fancy way you talk in class."

"What fancy—"

"I'm tellin him, if you don't mind, Brian."

"Tell him then."

"He don't like the way you say 'tennis shoes' instead of sneakers. He don't like coloreds. A whole bunch a things, really."

"I never done nothing to him. He's got no reason—"

"*And*," said Nailor, grinning, "*and*, he says you're a stuck-up rich kid." Nailor's eyes had crow's-feet, bags beneath them. They were a man's eyes.

"My dad's a sergeant," I said.

"You chicken to fight him?" said Nailor.

"Yeah, Clint, don't be chicken. Jest go on and git it over with. He's whupped pert near ever'body else in the class. It ain't so bad."

"Might as well, Oates."

"Yeah, yer pretty skinny, but yer jest about his height. Jest git 'im in a headlock and don't let go."

"Goddamn," I said, "he's got no reason to—"

Their eyes shot right and I looked over my shoulder. Oakley stood at his locker, turning its tumblers. From where I stood I could see that a piece of cotton was wedged up one of his nostrils, and he already had the makings of a good shiner. His acne burned red like a fresh abrasion. He snapped the locker open and kicked his shoes off without sitting. Then he pulled off his shorts, revealing two paddle stripes on his ass. They were fresh red bars speckled with white, the white speckles being the reverse impression of the paddle's suction holes. He must not have watched his filthy mouth while in Gilchrest's presence. Behind me, I heard Preston and Nailor pad to their lockers.

Oakley spoke without turning around. "Somebody's gonna git his skinny black ass kicked, right today, right after school." He said it softly. He slipped his jock off, turned around, his hairy nakedness a weapon clearing the younger boys from his path. Just before he rounded the corner of the shower stalls, I threw my toliet kit to the floor and stammered, "I—I never did nothing to you, Oakley." He stopped, turned, stepped closer to me, wrapping his towel around himself. Sweat streamed down my rib cage. It felt like ice water. "You wanna go at it right now, boy?"

"I never did nothing to you." I felt tears in my eyes. I couldn't stop them even though I was blinking like mad. "Never."

He laughed. "You busted my nose, asshole."

"What about before? What I'd ever do to you?"

"See you after school, Coonie." Then he turned away, flashing his acne-spotted back like a semaphore. "Why?" I shouted. "Why you wanna fight me?" Oakley stopped and turned, folded his arms, leaned against a toilet stall. "Why you wanna fight *me*, Oakley?" I stepped over the bench. "What'd I do? Why me?" And then unconsciously, as if scratching, as if breathing, I walked toward Marvin, who stood a few feet from Oakley, combing his hair at the mirror. "Why not him?" I said. "How come you're after *me* and not *him*?" The room froze. Froze for a moment that was both evanescent and eternal, somewhere between an eye blink and a week in hell. No one moved, nothing happened; there was no sound at all. And then it was as if all of us at the same moment looked at Marvin. He just stood there, combing away, the only body in motion, I think. He combed his hair and combed it, as if seeing only his image, hearing only his comb scraping his scalp. I knew he'd heard me. There was no way he could not have heard me. But all he did was slide the comb into his pocket and walk out the door.

"I got no quarrel with Marvin," I heard Oakley say. I turned toward his voice, but he was already in the shower.

I was able to avoid Oakley at the end of the school day. I made my escape by asking Mrs. Wickham if I could go to the rest room.

" 'Rest room,' " Oakley mumbled. "It's a damn toilet, sissy."

"Clinton," said Mrs. Wickham. "Can you *not* wait till the bell rings? It's almost three o'clock."

"No ma'am," I said. "I won't make it."

"Well, I should make you wait just to teach you to be more mindful about . . . hygiene . . . uh, things." She sucked in her cheeks, squinted. "But I'm feeling charitable today. You may go." I immediately left the building, and got on the bus. "Ain't you a little early?" said the bus driver, swinging the door shut. "Just left the office," I said. The driver nodded, apparently not giving me a second thought. I had no idea why I'd told her I'd come from the office, or why she found it a satisfactory answer. Two minutes later the bus filled, rolled, and shook its way to Connolly Air Base. When I got home, my mother was sitting in the living room, smoking her Slims, watching her soap opera. She absently asked me how my day had gone and I told her fine. "Hear from Dad?" I said.

"No, but I'm sure he's fine." She always said that when we hadn't heard from him in a while. I suppose she thought I was worried about him, or that I felt vulnerable without him. It was neither. I just wanted to discuss something with my mother that we both cared about. If I spoke with her about things that happened in school, or on my weekends, she'd listen with half an ear, say something like, "Is that so?" or "You don't say?" I couldn't stand that sort of thing. But when I mentioned my father, she treated me a bit more like an adult, or at least someone who was worth listening to. I didn't want to feel like a boy that afternoon. As I turned from my mother and walked down the hall, I thought about the day my father left for Viet Nam. Sharp in his uniform, sure behind his aviator specs, he slipped a cigar from his pocket and stuck it in mine. "Not till I get back," he said. "We'll have us one when we go fishing. Just you and me, out on the lake all day, smoking and casting and sitting. Don't let Mama see it. Put it in y'back pocket." He hugged me, shook my hand, and told me I was the man of the house now. He told me he was depending on me to take good care of my mother and sister. "Don't you let me down, now, hear?" And he tapped his thick finger on my chest. "You almost as big as me. Boy, you something else." I believed him when he told me those things. My heart swelled big enough to swallow my father, my mother, Claire. I loved, feared, and respected myself, my manhood. That day I could have put all of Waco, Texas, in my heart. And it wasn't till about three months later that I discovered I really wasn't the man of the house, that my mother and sister, as they always had, were taking care of me.

For a brief moment I considered telling my mother about what had happened at school that day, but for one thing, she was deep down in the halls of *General Hospital*, and never paid much mind till it was over. For another thing, I just wasn't the kind of person—I'm still not, really—to discuss my problems with anyone. Like my father I kept things to myself, talked about my problems only in retrospect. Since my father wasn't around I consciously wanted to be like him, doubly like him, I could say. I wanted to be the man of the house in some respect, even if it had to be in an inward way. I went to my room, changed my clothes, and laid out my homework. I couldn't focus on it. I thought about Marvin, what I'd said about him or done to him—I couldn't tell which. I'd done something to him, said something about him; said something about and done something to myself. *How come you're after* me *and not* him? I kept trying to tell myself I hadn't meant it that way. *That* way. I thought about approaching Marvin, telling him what I really meant was that he was more Oakley's age and weight than I. I would tell him I meant I was no match for Oakley. *See, Marvin, what I meant was that he wants to fight a colored guy, but if afraid to fight you 'cause you could beat him.* But try as I did, I couldn't for a moment convince myself that Marvin would believe me. I meant it *that* way and no other. Everybody heard. Everybody knew. That afternoon I forced myself to confront the notion that tomorrow I would probably have to fight both Oakley and Marvin. I'd have to be two men.

I rose from my desk and walked to the window. The light made my skin look orange, and I started thinking about what Wickham had told us once about light. She said that oranges and apples, leaves and flowers, the whole multicolored world, was not what it appeared to be. The colors we see, she said, look like they do only because of the light or ray that shines on them. "The color of the thing isn't what you see, but the light that's reflected off it." Then she shut out the lights and shone a white light lamp on a prism. We watched the pale splay of colors on the projector screen; some people oohed and aahed. Suddenly, she switched on a black light and the color of everything changed. The prism colors vanished, Wickham's arms were purple, the buttons of her dress were as orange as hot coals, rather than the blue they had been only seconds before. We were all very quiet. "Nothing," she said, after a while, "is really what it appears to be." I didn't really understand then. But as I stood at the window, gazing at my orange skin, I wondered what kind of light I could shine on Marvin, Oakley, and me that would reveal us as the same.

I sat down and stared at my arms. They were dark brown again. I worked up a bit of saliva under my tongue and spat on my left arm. I spat again, then rubbed the spittle into it, polishing, working till my arm grew warm. As I spat, and rubbed, I wondered why Marvin did this weird, nasty thing to himself, day after day. Was he trying to rub away the black, or deepen it, doll it up? And if he did this weird nasty thing for a hundred years, would he spit-shine himself invisible, rolling away the eggplant skin, revealing the scarlet muscle, blue vein, pink and yellow tendon, white bone? Then disappear? Seen through, all colors, no colors. Spitting and rubbing. Is this the way you do it? I leaned forward, sniffed the arm. It smelled vaguely of mayonnaise. After an hour or so, I fell asleep.

I saw Oakley the second I stepped off the bus the next morning. He stood outside the gym in his usual black penny loafers, white socks, high-water jeans, t-shirt, and black jacket. Nailor stood with him, his big teeth spread across his bottom lip like playing cards. If there was anyone I felt like fighting, that day, it was Nailor. But I wanted to put off fighting for as long as I could. I stepped toward the gymnasium, thinking that I shouldn't run, but if I hurried I could beat Oakley to the door and secure myself near Gilchrest's office. But the moment I stepped into the gym, I felt Oakley's broad palm clap down on my shoulder. "Might as well stay out here, Coonie," he said. "I need me a little target practice." I turned to face him and he slapped me, one-two, with the back, then the palm of his hand, as I'd seen Bogart do to Peter Lorre in *The Maltese Falcon*. My heart went wild. I could scarcely breathe. I couldn't swallow.

"Call me a nigger," I said. I have no idea what made me say this. All I know is that it kept me from crying. "Call me a nigger, Oakley."

"Fuck you, ya black-ass slope." He slapped me again, scratching my eye. "I don't do what coonies tell me."

"Call me a nigger."

"Outside, Coonie."

"Call me one. Go ahead!"

He lifted his hand to slap me again, but before his arm

could swing my way, Marvin Pruitt came from behind me and calmly pushed me aside. "Git out my way, boy," he said. And he slugged Oakley on the side of his head. Oakley stumbled back, stiff-legged. His eyes were big. Marvin hit him twice more, once again to the side of the head, once to the nose. Oakley went down and stayed down. Though blood was drawn, whistles blowing, fingers pointing, kids hollering, Marvin just stood there, staring at me with cool eyes. He spat on the ground, licked his lips, and just stared at me, till Coach Gilchrest and Mr. Calderon tackled him and violently carried him away. He never struggled, never took his eyes off me.

Nailor and Mrs. Wickham helped Oakley to his feet. His already fattened nose bled and swelled so that I had to look away. He looked around, bemused, walleyed, maybe scared. It was apparent he had no idea how bad he was hurt. He didn't blink. He didn't even touch his nose. He didn't look like he knew much of anything. He looked at me, looked me dead in the eye, in fact, but didn't seem to recognize me.

That morning, like all other mornings, we said the Pledge of Allegiance, sang "The Yellow Rose of Texas," "The Eyes of Texas Are upon You," and "Mistress Shady." The room stood strangely empty without Oakley, and without Marvin, but at the same time you could feel their presence more intensely somehow. I felt like I did when I'd walk into my mother's room and could smell my father's cigars or cologne. He was more palpable, in certain respects, than when there in actual flesh. For some reason, I turned to look at Ah-so, and just this once I let my eyes linger on her face. She had a very gentle-looking face, really. That surprised me. She must have felt my eyes on her because she glanced up at me for a second and smiled, white teeth, downcast eyes. Such a pretty smile. That surprised me too. She held it for a few seconds, then let it fade. She looked down at her desk, and sat still as a photograph.

# Playing the Garden

## CHRIS FISHER

I can't understand the way some people's heads work. Mom has explained to me that if everyone thought the same, it would be a dull world. Dad disagrees. He thinks if everything were done his way, the world would run a lot more smoothly. I've been trying to figure things out by myself lately, watching people, deciding what makes them tick. Mom says I should stop staring.

Everything looked pretty rosy in the fall. I was heading into grade eleven and the twins, Kathryn and Kevin, were enrolled at the University of Saskatchewan in Saskatoon. Kevin, the southwest's best hockey prospect since Brian Trottier hitchhiked out of Val Marie, was going to play with the university hockey team. There had been some heavy talks around the kitchen table about that decision. Dad was positive that the road to success lay with the Regina Pats, the junior club that held Kevin's rights. After countless examples, Kevin finally convinced him that National Hockey League scouts watched university games, too.

The city is a four-hour drive north from the farm, so Dad rented the twins a three-bedroom house close to the university. They came home every weekend. The very first time Kathryn came home alone, even as she walked in the door and said Kevin had stayed in the city, I had a feeling something wasn't right. They aren't identical twins, they don't know what each other's thinking or weird stuff like that, but they usually traveled together.

Kevin is the oldest, three minutes ahead of Kathryn and eighteen months ahead of me. Being so close in age, Kevin and I did a lot together growing up. Dad claims that Kevin could have said he was hitchhiking to the North Pole and I'd have followed him out the door in my shorts. Sometimes during a game I would just lean back and watch him, pretending it was me scoring the goal or, for two months in the summer, pitching no-hitters and hitting the ball over the fence.

Kathryn and I spent our growing up time fighting. Mom says I pick on Kathryn because I'm jealous that she is Kevin's twin and I'm just a brother. That's too deep for me. I think anybody with a spaced-out sister like Kathryn would have to occasionally drag her back down to earth.

The second weekend in a row that Kathryn came home alone, everyone became suspicious. She said she was working on a psychology assignment, interpreting a dream of a member of the opposite sex. Since she wasn't dating anyone, proving to me that those university guys really were bright, she came home looking for a "male study." She asked Dad on Saturday morning, at breakfast, if he would participate. He said the only dreams he ever remembered were of tractors and grasshoppers, and even Hectare our cat could figure that out.

"Get Kevin to help," he said.

Kathryn and Mom exchanged looks. They knew something, that was for sure.

Mom said in her cheery, early morning voice that drives me nuts, "I imagine Kevin has enough to do. More bacon?"

Dad ignored the plate Mom was holding out and looked from Kathryn to her and back again.

"Why not him? Won't he have the same assignment?"

Kathryn shrugged. "Not sure. Different classes."

Dad pushed his plate away and leaned his forearms on the table. "You started in the same classes, didn't you?"

Kathryn nodded.

"Now you're in different classes."

She nodded, glancing again at Mom.

"Same university?"

"Yes."

"Still living in the same house?" Dad asked.

"Of course, Daddy. It's just that he's not around a lot. He hangs out with different people."

I could understand that. Kevin had met some people with good taste who only associated with quality women.

Dad nodded and pointed at me.

"Check out this dreamer," he growled, waving his half-eaten piece of toast at me. "See what button we have to push to get a little work out of him."

He had been upset with me ever since I told him I wasn't going to follow in his farmer footsteps, and I should spend next summer with Kevin in Saskatoon, looking for a part-time job. He said I would stay at home and earn my keep.

I didn't see any harm in helping Kathryn out. I remembered one dream I'd had pretty steady for the last few years, "recurring" is what Kathryn called it, and I thought it might be interesting to see what she came up with.

"Okay," I told her, "I'll do it on one condition. No smart-ass comments while I'm talking, and after it's done, you tell me what you wrote."

"That's two conditions."

"Your future's definitely in the math field," I said. "Is it a deal or not? I've got other things to do."

She agreed; the report was due next week. We went into the living room and she told me to lie down on the couch. She dragged over the big recliner-rocker and sat down, holding a pen and paper. Then she leaned over the coffee table and flicked on her tape recorder.

"Now," she said, clearing her throat, "Case A, begin your dream dialogue."

"Okay, I started having this dream six years ago and—"

"Six? Are you positive? Why would you remember that?"

"I remember because our peewee team had just won provincials. Our deal was you wouldn't cut in."

"You mean after Kevin won."

I glared at her. One of Kathryn's most annoying habits is in stating the obvious. Everyone knew that Kevin was our whole team. He could have won with just himself and a goalie. We won the final 6–3 and he scored five of the goals. I got the other one. I fell in front of their net and the puck deflected off my helmet. I consider myself a positional player.

"Sorry," I said. "I didn't realize you were telling this. Carry on, I'm curious about how it ends."

That shut her up. She zipped her mouth closed and motioned for me to continue. I leaned back and looked up at the ceiling so I could pretend she didn't exist.

"The New York Rangers are scouting for a center-man. They're Kevin's favorite team. Funny, though, it's my dream and I'm a Leaf fan. You'd think . . . " I could hear her pen scratching away by my ear. "Anyway, it's a Ranger scout watching us skate down at the Garden."

The Garden is our nickname for the rink Dad makes each year down behind the garage. He smooths out Mom's potato patch, puts up some plywood boards and floods until there's enough ice to skate on. It's our job to keep the ice clean of snow.

"This scout comes into the garage where Kevin and I are taking our skates off. He's got this million-dollar contract and a big pen with a fancy feather plume on it. He waves it at Kevin and says, 'Sign here, my boy.' Kevin says, 'No way, José, not without my right-winger.' He points at me. The two of us are a unit, a package deal. Playing without me would be like playing with one skate. The scout winks at me and agrees. He pulls out another contract that I sign with a Bic."

Kathryn interrupted again.

"Do you recognize the scout?"

"Yeah, it's Fred Flintstone."

She started to scratch that down.

"No, I was joking, I was kidding. The scout isn't familiar."

She sighed and said, "Continue," real professional, like it was me who stopped in the first place.

"We immediately fly to New York for their next NHL game. There's cameras flashing and reporters scurrying around. We rush to Madison Square Garden, where a huge crowd's milling around out front. They sneak us in a side door. The players are in Ranger uniforms but they're all my favorites, Davey Keon and Paul Henderson and Bobby Orr and Anders Hedberg. They shake our hands and look relieved, like the U. S. cavalry just arrived. We get brand-new skates and as many sticks and rolls of tape as we want." I stopped, trying to find the right words. I had never explained the dream to anyone before, just lived and felt the scenes.

"There's got to be more," Kathryn said. "It has to be a ten-page report."

"Well, the opposition's never very clear, like it's not Montreal one night and Boston the next. And the players are kind of fuzzy, with no real shape to them. There's this mist clinging to everything, like fog. Our whole team, except me and Kevin, sits on the bench. The stands are a big blur, but I can hear the crowd roaring, the rise and fall of the noise as the play develops. Whenever I look up, there's Kevin, either giving me a great pass or in perfect position to catch one. We weave through everybody."

I stopped, realizing something about the dream that I'd never noticed before. "It's weird, but we never finish the season, never play for the Stanley Cup. There's just miles to skate, goals to score, games to play forever. There's no end, just this feeling, this satisfaction, making the good play and knowing it's a good play and being . . . being . . . "

"Appreciated?"

"Yeah, that's the word, appreciated. You know what I mean?"

"I know the term, not the feeling." Kathryn stopped scratching on the paper and sighed. "Is that all?"

"Tha-tha-tha that's all, folks," I answered, sitting up.

Kathryn clicked off the tape recorder and gathered it up. She retreated into her room and shut the door, leaving her Garfield Do Not Disturb sign around the knob. At supper-time, Mom knocked on her door and went in. She stayed in there for almost an hour and came out alone. By then the potatoes were cold and Dad wouldn't eat because Hockey Night in Canada had already started. Mom seemed quieter than usual and went to bed early.

On Sunday morning, after a night of tapping away on the typewriter, the hermit emerged from her cave. She sat down at the breakfast table all smiles and didn't say a word.

"Well," I finally asked, "what's the verdict?"

"Hero worship," she announced, as proud as if she had just spouted off $E=mc^2$.

"Deep," I said, looking across the table at Dad.

"She'll go far," he said.

Mom broke in. "Very good work, dear. I'm sure Kevin will be pleased his brother admires him."

"Right, Mom," Kathryn said, and they exchanged another glance.

Dad noticed the look and thumped his cup down so hard that the coffee slopped onto the table. "What's going on here? Am I going to miss another meal before I find out anything? You and Kevin not talking?"

"We talk."

"What's up, then? You come home without him, someone's changing classes, you don't see him much. Is homework affecting his workouts? Should he cut his workload? Too many parties? Girls? Should I call his coach or what?"

When Dad hollers, we listen.

"Kevin should be telling you this," Kathryn said. "But since you insist, he's decided not to play hockey this year."

"Aha! I told him junior was better for him but would he listen? No. Now their season's started already. Has he talked to the Pats coach yet? Never mind, I'll call Jamieson right away. God knows he's called me enough over the years."

"Dad, he's—"

"That explains why he hasn't been home. His pride's been hurt, hates to admit I was right all along. Well, I'll call him, too, once I find out some news from the Pats."

Dad started to get up, to move toward the phone.

Mom reached over and put her hand on his shoulder. "Frank, he's not playing at all, anywhere, period."

Dad sat back down with a thump.

Someone had to have their wires crossed somewhere. Maybe I would end up playing right wing for the Dolguard Seniors but Kevin was different. He was going places, places for me, for all of us. Some day we'd watch him live in the Stanley Cup, or huddle around the TV on Saturday night and cheer when he was the first star.

Dad took a gulp of his coffee, swished it around in his mouth and swallowed. "If this is some practical joke, I'm telling you right now, I'm not laughing."

"It's the truth, Dad," Kathryn said. "They've started practicing and he hasn't gone. I shouldn't say anything. He would have told you when it was time."

"Maybe he'll change his mind," I suggested.

They all turned and stared at me.

"Well, what's his problem?" Dad asked.

"Dad, maybe he should tell you—"

"What's his prob-lem!" he hollered.

"It takes up too much time. His heart's not in it. He says he's had enough of hockey and now there's other things to do. He's got other interests, things he's never done before." Kathryn stood up. "He's switching classes, taking drama, going from education to arts."

Once, in grade eight, I was wrestling Ned Parker, my best friend, and he kicked me in the nuts. The pain didn't hurt as much as the surprise that he would even think of doing that to me. I felt that same emptiness now.

Mom stood up and started clearing off the dishes, even though no one had finished eating. "It'll straighten itself out. There's obviously been some mix-up. Frank, calm down. No use getting excited over something we can't change." She wiped up the coffee that Dad had spilled.

"I am calm, dammit. Kathryn, is there a girl?"

"Not that I know of. I told you, he hangs around with a group of guys."

"And they're not from the hockey team?" Dad asked.

Kathryn looked uncomfortable and Mom coughed.

"No," Kathryn said.

Mom moved to stand behind Dad's chair. She put her hand on his shoulder.

"Well, that's it," Dad said. "Years down the tube. Move to the city, get a little freedom, get into trouble."

"Oh, no," Kathryn said. "Kevin isn't in any trouble."

"Wasn't, you mean. Tell him he can stay away if he wants to. He made his own bed, now he can sleep in it."

Dad rose from the table and stomped into the living room. He turned on the TV and slammed back into the recliner.

Mom was looking out the kitchen window. Kathryn moved over beside her.

"I had to tell him that at least, Mom," Kathryn said.

"He'd have found out as soon as they played their first game."

"Maybe, dear. I still think it might all blow over."

"None of this is blowing over, Mom."

Mom turned and looked into Kathryn's eyes and they did that thing I always hate, when they stare at each other as if they are peering into each other's souls. It seems to calm them down so I never tease them about it. I just sat at the table, not really thinking anything.

Mom sat down at the table beside me while Kathryn poured them both some tea. She lifted the pot toward me but I shook my head. I thought I should get up and start chores before Dad yelled. Kathryn came around and sat down on my other side. She leaned in and looked across at Mom.

"It's not the time or place," Mom said.

"When is?" Kathryn asked. "When he hears it at school? Or when he goes up and visits?"

Mom shrugged. "Are we the ones to tell him?"

"Probably not," Kathryn said. "But I'd want to be told by someone here, and not on the street. We're all family."

Mom sighed. "It's not for sure."

"Mom, I live with him. You don't know how many times I've told myself the same thing."

I sat listening to the conversation bounce back and forth and felt like I was watching a tennis match. An annoying tennis match, because I hadn't asked to watch.

"What are you two talking about?" I asked. "If you're talking about telling me, Kathryn, then there's nothing you could tell me more surprising than what you already have."

So, with Mom sitting beside me there, just staring into her tea, Kathryn told me.

It's been six weeks now and there is still a tenseness in the air around home. Kevin has yet to make an appearance but

Kathryn fills us in on his activities. She and I have had a couple of good talks, and I think she may turn out to be all right after all. Mom's been up to visit once but Dad wouldn't go. Mom asked if I wanted to go along, she said it was okay to miss school, but I had this biology project to work on. Mom sighed and gave me her sad look as I turned away. She knows how much I usually love an excuse to skip biology.

I'd had everybody in the world ask me if the rumors about Kevin are true. I knot up inside and ask, What rumors? They look at me kind of funny and say they heard that Kevin wasn't playing hockey. I say, I don't know, I haven't talked to him lately. The day the question changes, I don't know what or how I'll answer.

Every year for as long as I can remember we've spent the end of December flooding the Garden and building a respectable rink. Dad started early this year, clearing and raking the surface. He hasn't asked for my help or even mentioned that he's started. He put the boards up himself while I was at school. It hasn't been nearly cold enough, but he's been flooding every night after "The Journal," almost willing the water to freeze. I'm sure he's trying to have it ready by next weekend, when the twins come home for Christmas break.

I'm nervous about seeing Kevin but keep telling myself that he'll look and act the same and so should I. Mom says Dad will behave himself but Dad says a guy can do whatever he wants in his own house. I imagine that Dad plans on taking Kevin down to the rink for a chat, hoping that the magic of the Garden will transform Kevin into having the desire to play hockey again. Kevin will then tell Dad what the rest of us already know. Mom and Kathryn will busy themselves making another large meal and I'll go and do the chores early.

Of course I know Dad's dreaming, and I certainly don't believe in magic, but for the past two mornings I've been up at five. The ground is still wet and soft, and it's hardly cold enough for you to see your breath. I flood anyway, trying to step in Dad's tracks so he doesn't know I've been down there. The weatherman said temperatures could drop to ten below tonight. Maybe we'll get ice after all. If blood is truly thicker than water, even the frozen, then the healing will have to start down at the Garden.

# The White Room

REBECCA RULE

The dead tree, a stump really, was unusual because it had three limbs intact, still sturdy and reaching for the sky. The bark was gone, the wood bleached white and purified by wind, rain, sun; the grain stood distinct, textured. Driftwood on the river bank, high and dry now that the water was down for the summer. Marie enlisted her Uncle Octave to help drag the tree back to the house.

It took a deal of manipulation to get it up the stairs to the second floor. He had to take the door from its hinges and maneuver the limbs just so into the white room where they both pushed hard until it wedged tight ceiling-to-floor, not to be moved again without a crowbar. Once in place, the tree looked as though it had grown there.

Uncle Octave clapped his hands at a job well done. He danced and chanted. There was Abenaki blood in the family—but Marie didn't suppose he was performing an authentic dance: he'd just invented one to make her smile. Octave was the clown among her mother's five brothers— all of whom had come home for her funeral, four of whom had already disappeared again into the world.

The most musically talented of the LaVallee brothers, Octave was a song-and-dance man who played squeeze-box, harmonica, banjo, and, sometimes, guitar. He could also tap-dance, juggle, walk on his hands, touch the tip of his nose with his tongue, and flap his tongue like bird wings.

Marie knew that eventually he too would disappear into the world—leaving her alone in the house when Pepère was away, alone in the dark when Pepère worked the night train or had a Boston layover. But for now, Octave slept in the small room behind the kitchen and Marie slept better knowing he was there: the house was a big one, and—though she had lived in it all her life—there were nooks, stairwells, trapdoors, and shadows that frightened her, but mostly the white room.

"This will be a safe place for animals," she told Octave, having devised big plans: fallen birds nurtured to maturity, cat-wounded chipmunks restored to health, a colony of painted turtles, frogs from the backwater, mice live-trapped and caged out of harm's way, barn spiders in each corner. The tree would be the centerpiece for her menagerie.

When she told her mother how the white room frightened her, Mother said: "Then it is yours."

"I won't sleep in it," Marie said. "I won't sleep in that creepy place." The walls were smooth plaster and the two small windows faced evergreen woods pressed to the north corner of the house.

"Not to sleep in," her mother said. "You have your bedroom for sleeping. This will be a room for play and adventure."

"I don't want it," Marie said.

Mother brought out the sketchbook. "The ceiling will be the sky," she said. "Fair weather clouds"—she traced them with charcoal pencil—"and color." With her palette knife she mixed and spread three distinct blues. "A sky full of color," she said, daubing pink-blue, silver-blue, and lavender.

"And the walls," she said, "how shall we paint your walls? The ocean? The desert? A field of wildflowers."

"Yes, the ocean," Marie agreed. But a calm ocean with mist rising, an ocean so tame a girl could easily spot the black head of a seal. And for the other walls—scenes she knew: the sandbar in the river where the birches hung low; the apple tree when the grass was high and the black-eyed susans blooming; the shining granite ledge among the hemlock.

Mother sketched each scene. "Use the pastels to suggest the colors," she said. But Marie was afraid she'd ruin the pictures. Though she loved to draw and paint, though she spent many hours alongside her mother working with pencil, pastels, water colors, even oils, Marie's pictures were—to her own eye—never good enough. Her mother's pictures were round, living—inviting a person to step in and find a world.

"All right then," Mother compromised, "you tell me which colors and where." Marie pressed the pastel sticks one at a time into her mother's open, steady hand.

They could not start painting the walls themselves until they had the proper paint, and plenty of it. Pepère agreed to buy the paint for them in Boston when he had to stay the night on layover.

The first week he brought home forest green and pale yellow. The second week it was cherry red and sapphire blue. A quart of each, week after week until the closet floor was cobbled with paint cans. They would start the project as soon as all the paint was assembled. They would start when Mother felt better.

But she only felt worse. Her hands shook. Her eyes sank. She couldn't lift her head from the pillow. Then she died. The brothers whirled in and filled the house. Pepère sat silent in the big chair, surrounded by his noisy sons. He couldn't keep his hands still. Tap, tap on the arm of the chair. Tap, tap. Tap, tap. Marie watched from a silence of her own. All these strangers in the house—Babineau, Arthur, Emery, Louis, and Octave. Soon, only Octave remained.

More than anything, Marie wanted a squirrel for the tree in the white room. A family of red squirrels lived in the stonewall along the garden. The cat had already caught and killed two of them. Marie wanted to capture and tame one—to save it from the cat, which would get them all eventually; he was a hunter, that fellow.

The squirrel would live in the white room and make it the happy place her mother had intended. Marie had found a small turtle and built a box home for it in one corner, but that slow, quiet life had failed to drive the creepy feelings away. A squirrel was called for—lively and mischievous— to cause all manner of havoc: a pet as quick and irreverent as Uncle Octave himself.

Marie lured the squirrels with sunflower seeds. She noted favorite exit holes among the stones and positioned herself, like the cat, in pouncing position. It was a long wait, all one afternoon, while Pepère was away at work— riding the train to somewhere and back—and Octave practiced banjo on the porch. She waited and watched, her legs cramping under her, mosquitoes drilling her flesh, pine odors rising when the sun baked the needles, the clouds moving in the sky.

The first time a squirrel head poked out of the hole, she did not move—but her whole body went on alert and her hands curled in readiness. Next, when the squirrel poked all the way out, Marie grabbed for it and caught fur. Her hand closed around the squirming body and held firm even when the tiny teeth sank deep and the blood came.

She held on and ran for the house yelling, "Open the door, open the door!" Octave held the screen as she whirled through, up the stairs and into the white room, kicking the door shut behind her. Then she shook the squirrel off. He found his legs, zoomed up the tree and stood on the highest limb screaming.

Octave slipped into the room before she could say close the door.

"What the hyde is going on?" he said.

"I caught a squirrel," she said, "for my tree. I told you I wanted a squirrel and a bird and a rabbit and spiders."

He said: "You have blood all over yourself."

Her arm was slick with it, her shirt badly stained, her hand throbbing. The pain made her sit down quick on the floor.

Octave brought a wet rag and washed the blood away. The squirrel had located a window and was clawing the glass. He ran around the room once, testing every corner. He ran over Marie's foot, then back up the tree.

Octave made her drink a glass of water. She watched the squirrel racing back and forth on the limb. Octave smeared her hand with stinging medicine and wrapped it gently. "Hurt like Hades," he said. "Just so it doesn't get infected!"

"I grabbed him and he bit me, but I wouldn't let go," she said. "I figured he could bite me and make me let go and I'd be bitten for nothing; or I could just hold on. So I did."

They sat side by side on the floor. Uncle Octave's legs were not much longer than her own—and he was a grown man, but a small one, the smallest of the brothers, light enough to ride across the field on Babineau's shoulders.

"I think the squirrel will need a cage until it's tamed," she said.

"I can build a cage," Octave said. "I will do that for you."

"Yes," she said. "If I sketch it—will you build it just the way I want it to be?"

"How do you want it to be, Marie?" he teased.

She found the sketchbook in the closet, turned quickly past the sketches her mother had made—the sky, the ocean, the sandbar, the apple tree, the granite ledge—to a blank page near the end. The bandage made it awkward—but not impossible—to hold the charcoal. Her hand hurt, but all the fingers moved.

But before she could draw a line, Octave lifted her hand from the page and placed it on her knee. "Let's see," he said, turning back to the color sketches, examining them one by one.

"Did you draw these, Marie?"

She shook her head. "We were going to paint these pictures on the walls," she said. "Pepère bought the paint and everything."

"Then it should be done," he said. "Definitely."

He laid the sketch of the ocean on the floor in front of them. "Stare at it," he said. "Take it into your heart."

They stared at it together for a long, long time—the grays and blues and whites, the tinges of pink and yellow. She saw how the colors fit together like clasped hands, how they balanced the smooth, black head of the seal.

When Marie raised her head, she saw the picture transposed on the white wall, projected there—huge and in full color.

"I see it," she said. "There, on the wall. Can you?"

"Paint it," he said. "Paint what you see."

"But it's all there," she said. "All that's left is to mix the colors and fill them in where they go. That's too easy," she said. "That's not fair."

"It's your mother's gift," he said. "Accept it."

By first frost, the squirrel was eating from Marie's scarred hand and chattering from her shoulder. Octave had returned to the world, but promised to visit at Christmas. The white room was no longer white. When Marie ran out of walls to paint, she worked on canvas. She painted every day. She painted the life she knew.

Babineau, home to help shingle the barn roof, observed that Marie was even more talented than her mother had been. Pepère nearly struck him when he said that. But deep down Pepère knew—they all knew—that Marie's was a gift that could not be contained.

## BIOGRAPHICAL NOTES ON THE AUTHORS

SANDRA CISNEROS lives in San Antonio, Texas, and is the author of the novels *The House on Mango Street* and *Caramelo;* a collection of short stories, *Woman Hollering Creek;* and two volumes of poetry. She has won many awards, including a MacArthur Foundation Fellowship, a Before Columbus Foundation American Book Award, and two fellowships from The National Endowment for the Arts. Her books have been translated into more than a dozen languages.

RAND RICHARDS COOPER is author of the novels *The Last to Go* and *Big as Life*. His fiction has been read on NPR's "Selected Shorts," and has been published in *Harper's*, *The Atlantic, Esquire,* and other magazines. His story, "Johnny Hamburger," was published in *Best American Short Stories* (2003). Cooper is a contributing editor at *Bon Appétit*. He lives in Hartford, Connecticut.

CHRIS FISHER is the author of two short fiction collections, *Sun Angel,* winner of the Saskatchewan Book Award, and *Voices in the Wilderness*. His stories have been widely published in literary periodicals and anthologies, including *Coming Attractions*, an influential anthology series of new Canadian writers, and in *Show Me a Hero: Great Contemporary Stories About Sports*. He lives in Saskatchewan, Canada.

K. KVASHAY-BOYLE'S stories have been published in *McSweeney's, Better of McSweeney's, The Best American Non-Required Reading, Politically Inspired Fiction,* and other literary journals. She is a graduate of the Iowa Writers' Workshop, and was recently nominated for a Pushcart Prize. "Saint Chola" was her first published story, written for her best friend: the admirable and triumphant Summra Shariff. She lives in Los Angeles, California.

WALLY LAMB is a native of Norwich, Connecticut. His novels *She's Come Undone* and *I Know This Much Is True* were each chosen as a *New York Times Book Review* Notable Book, as Oprah Book Club selections, and each novel reached number one on the *New York Times* bestsellers list.

CAITLIN JEFFREY LONNING lives in Connecticut. She wrote this story when she was a fifteen-year-old junior in high school. She now studies at Washington University in St. Louis, Missouri, where she was awarded the Nemerov Prize for creative writing.

SANDELL MORSE lives in York, Maine. Her work has appeared in *Ploughshares, New England Review, Green Mountains Review,* and in the anthology *Surviving Crisis: Twenty Prominent Authors Write About Events that Shaped Their Lives.* She has been a Tennessee Williams Scholar at the Sewanee Writers' Conference and a fellow at the Virginia Center for the Creative Arts. She has also been nominated for a Pushcart Prize.

KATHARINE NOEL lives in San Francisco, California, and teaches at Stanford University, where she held Wallace Stegner and Truman Capote fellowships. She is the author of a novel, *Halfway House.*

CLAIRE ROBSON is a British-born writer who lived in the United States for fifteen years before moving to Vancouver, British Columbia. She has been a high school teacher, and has taught writing workshops for teenagers and adults. She is the author of the memoir *Love in Good Time,* as well as many poems and stories. Her work has appeared in numerous journals, including *North American Review, Orchid,* and *So to Speak.*

REBECCA RULE lives in Northwood, New Hampshire. Her short stories have been widely published and anthologized. She is the author of three collections, including *The Best Revenge* (which won the New Hampshire Writers Project Award for the best work of fiction), and, most recently, *Could Have Been Worse*. She is a columnist for the *Concord Monitor* (syndicated in the *Portsmouth Herald* and the *Nashua Telegraph*).

ANNETTE SANFORD lives in Ganardo, Texas. She has been awarded two fellowships from the National Endowment for the Arts, and has published two collections of short stories, *Lasting Attachments* and *Crossing Shattuck Bridge*. "Nobody Listens When I Talk" was included in *Best American Short Stories*.

AKHIL SHARMA lives in New York City. His novel *An Obedient Father* won the 2001 PEN/Hemingway Award and the Sue Kaufman Prize from the American Academy of Arts and Letters. His short stories have been published in *The Atlantic* and *The New Yorker*, and have been included in the both the *Best American Short Stories* and the O. Henry Award winners anthologies.

JACQUELINE SHEEHAN is a psychologist, fiction writer, and essayist. She has published an historical novel, *Truth*, about the life of Sojourner Truth. She frequently gives lectures based on her novel and also on the craft of writing. She is the fiction editor for *Patchwork Journal*, an on-line journal sponsored by Patchwork Farms, an international writing center. She leads writing workshops for Voices from Inside, a group that sponsors writing for women in prison. She lives in western Massachusetts.